Mama's Ring

Pamela Venn

All rights reserved. No part of this publication may be reproduced, stored in a retrieval system, or transmitted, in any form or by any means, electronic, mechanical, photocopying, recording, or otherwise, without the written prior permission of the author.

Copyright © 2016 by Pamela Venn
All rights reserved.

Green Ivy Publishing
1 Lincoln Centre
18W140 Butterfield Road
Suite 1500
Oakbrook Terrace IL 60181-4843
www.greenivybooks.com

Mama's Ring /Pamela Venn
ISBN: 978-1-9464-4632-9
Ebook: 978-1-9464-4633-6

This book is dedicated to my sister Evelyn Janice Griffin who helped me develop Earnestine. Janice lost her battle with lung cancer in 2010. See you later, sis.

JUST a LITTLE FAITH
When I woke this morning, the clouds were rolling in.
Storms of life were gathering at my door
Said a prayer to start my day
All those storm clouds rolled away
Just a little faith will make you strong
And drive away the storm.

Faith to keep you going on, faith to live and grow on
When you are down just have a little faith
Faith that you can hold onto
If you believe that GOD is true
Just a little faith will see you through.
Faith will see you through.

When the night brings darkness, the worries of the day
Become a raging river in my soul
I whisper, Lord, please lead me on.
Give me the faith to make me strong.
That river becomes a gentle stream
Becomes a gentle stream.

Prologue

Andrea slipped the ring from her finger and placed it, along with the letter and her journal, inside a small velvet bag. She tied the opening shut then sealed the string with wax and laid it aside to cool. She took a gold coin from the lining of her valise; it was the last one of the five she'd hidden there before leaving Paris. Then she placed both the velvet bag and the coin inside the bodice of her dress. When it became full light outside, she would find the trader from Charleston and ask him to send the letter to England. She could only hope that the ring would remind her daughter that she was always in her thoughts.

Judith shook her head in disbelief. "Get a life, Ida. I can't believe you're idolizing a woman who deserted her family, her kids for God's sake. If what you say about her is true, then she left her husband and kids to run with this count and his voodoo priestess friend. She was an adulteress. If she died while still in his company, I say good riddance."

Ida Mae looked at her as if she'd slapped her face. "Judith, don't be so judgmental. You seem to forget everybody's life is not as easy as yours has been," she snapped. Then she left the kitchen. Judith heard the front door close and, when she pulled back the curtain, she saw Ida Mae stuff her hands into the front pockets of her faded jean shorts as she walked past the edge of the driveway to the sidewalk.

It was Hattie Williams's first day on the street. Her first day as a homeless person. She bought a bagel with cream cheese in a small café then headed back onto the street. For the next ten hours, Hattie alternated between walking aimlessly and sitting, confused. She was scared and alone sitting on the curb or, whenever possible, a park bench. When nightfall came she found shelter behind a thick grouping of bushes in the city park. Before daylight her purse was gone. The thief had slipped up close to where Hattie slept, grabbed the purse, and run away. When Hattie awoke she was even more confused. She reached for her purse but found nothing. She was alone and broke.

Kathy shook her head. Tears formed in her eyes and spilled over and down her cheeks. She started to talk. "I killed my brother. I didn't mean to but it was my fault just the same. Sometimes I wanted him to go away, to just disappear but not usually. Usually I loved him. I was the only family he had, the only one who cared for him. Poor Cal. Poor sweet, dumb Cal."

Marita knew in her heart that everything she'd been told about her mother was a lie. She pulled her coat down from the peg and began digging in the pockets. That's where she'd hidden an apple and a cookie from the rescue mission. Since she'd used what little money she had left to buy heroin, she had no money for food, so she ate one hot meal at the center every day. She didn't go back for the evening meal. If you ate supper there, you were expected to listen to the preacher talk, so she didn't go back. That's why she always put something in her pocket to eat later.

Davis remembered his mama's words as clearly as if it were yesterday. "God made you for a purpose, son. I don't know what it is and, from the way you're living, I don't think you know either but, make no mistake, you have one. All this rushing about won't satisfy you no matter what you think. You won't have no peace till you find out what it is God has planned for you."

Joseph knew he was dying. Dying wasn't the problem. He knew Jesus had saved him. He knew that when his soul left his earthly body it would travel to where his savior was waiting. Jesus had said, "In my house are many mansions. I go to prepare a place for you so that where I am you may be also." Joseph was not afraid to die. Leaving his maw alone was the problem. Leaving his maw alone to worry about his burying was the problem. His maw had cried and fretted over friends and neighbors dead and gone without a proper burial. Friends gone with no songs sung or prayers prayed.

Harmon Presley was used to being called out on short notice." I've got all I need right here." He pulled his Bible out of his coat pocket." I'll follow you in my truck."

For the next four days, Harmon laid hands on Martha Gaines and prayed. He prayed till he was hoarse and exhausted. In the last hours of her life, she became lucid enough to call for her husband. She pleaded with him to care for her two boys' spiritual needs. "Please Zeb," she begged. "Please give up this feud you have with God and take my sons to church."

Zack's heart was beating so hard he could feel it in his head, drowning out every other sound. The September air was chilly but he began to sweat. Fear gripped his insides. His father's voice bounced around inside his head, competing with the thumping beat of his heart. "Lord, help me," he prayed silently." Don't let me shame myself in front of Gabe and Paw again." He watched his brother Gabe insert the pole under the rock. The rock began to rise off the ground. He sucked in his breath. Underneath the rock, a writhing mass of coils moved over and around each other, startled by the rock's movement. The loop from his paw's snake hook fell over one of the heads protruding from the mass. Suddenly one of the long bodies came free from the others and rose into the air, dangling from his father's snake hook.

Earnestine was scared, real scared, so scared she was sick to her stomach, but she was also excited. Earnestine kept telling herself she had nothing to be afraid of. After all, Maw had been learning her letters and counting and the spelling of her name. Not only that, Maw had promised her that the other kids would like her, so she'd surely have friends to play with. Her sixth birthday had passed three weeks earlier, and Maw had celebrated by making her a cinnamon sugar biscuit. That was real, real special.

Since then she had twice helped her maw load her year-old twin brothers into the makeshift cart and, with Earnestine leading four-year-old Burt and three-year-old Kate, they had made the long trek down the mountainside into town so that she would know how to get back and forth to school when the time came for her to make the trip alone.

Lester slipped along the side of the truck until he was directly behind Zebadiah Gaines. He raised the hammer then brought it down on the shoulder of Zebadiah's son Gabe. Gabe screamed in pain, twisting around and raising his arms in self-defense. As he did, his hand slipped from the sack and fell to the ground near his feet. The snakes wriggled and squirmed free of the sack and crawled toward where the boy lay.

MAMA'S RING

Pamela Doughty Venn

Love the Lord your God with all your heart and with all your soul and with all your mind. This is the first and greatest commandment and the second is like it. Love your neighbor as yourself.

Matthew 22:38–39

ANDREA BAKER 1800

Chapter 1

Andrea Justine Baker slumped slowly to the floor beside the bed and dropped her head forward in anguish. Her bronze hair was sticky with sweat and fell forward in wet strings. The air inside the hotel room was hot and muggy. She usually kept the window open to catch the evening breeze, but after last night it was closed and locked tight. Not that a locked window or door would keep the thing that was stalking her outside if it wanted to get in.

Andrea's tear-filled eyes fell on the ring she wore on her left hand. She caressed it, remembering when Reynaldo had given it to her. They had been seated in a small café in Paris when he'd placed it on her finger. They both knew they would never marry but, with the ring, Reynaldo had pledged his life to her.

The ring was gold with a large black diamond. It had been part of Reynaldo's family for over four hundred years. Reynaldo said the black diamond was the rarest and most coveted of all gemstones.

Could that have been only six short months ago? "Why did I insist on traveling to the West Indies?" she mumbled. "If only we had not gone to that cursed island. If only we had never boarded that vessel or listened to the corrupt counsel of Madam Devon. If, if, the world is filled with regrets and if's. I suppose many people will say I am deserving of whatever recompense I receive. No matter. There is naught I do but face it."

Andrea pulled herself to her feet, using the bedpost for support. She pushed strands of wet hair back from her face and straightened her back. "I am weary beyond belief!" she cried out loud. "I fear my transgressions have caught up to me. I coveted a man not my husband and I do not regret it. I have not deceived myself into believing I shan't pay the price." She crossed the room to where the blue enamel washbasin and pitcher sat atop a rickety wooden stand. She poured water from the pitcher into the enamel bowl, then cupped water in her hands and splashed it on her face. The water was warm but it did wonders to refresh her spirits.

Andrea dug through her valise and found her writing materials. She placed these onto the dark oak desk, not noticing the scratched and stained surface. She seated herself in the chair that she had pulled across the rough wooden floor to place near the desk. She opened the inkwell and placed her writing quill in the black ink. The paper had wrinkled inside the valise, so she smoothed out the wrinkles as best she could. This would doubtless be her last correspondence to her husband and children in England. She knew Joshua would be angry, not because he cared that she had deserted him but because her leaving had wounded his pride and caused him to be shamed in the eyes of his friends. She prayed he would set aside his pride long enough to read her letter.

She lifted the quill and blotted it carefully before

placing the tip to the paper.

Dear Joshua,

Please do not discard this letter without reading it. I will not insult you with an apology for my transgression. Truly I cannot say I feel sorry to have left although I am mindful of the grief I have caused. I am sorry for the shame I have caused you and my dear children. I know you never greatly loved me but I know you love Katherine and Jeremy and I know you will care for them.

I am not writing to ask for your help for I know that the adversary I now face is beyond help from any mortal. I am sending the one thing of value that I own and I ask that you hold it for Katherine and deliver it to her when she is old enough to be betrothed. For the sake of the love we both feel for our children, I pray that you will do this one thing for me.

Andrea Baker

Andrea slipped the ring from her finger and placed it, along with the letter and her journal, inside a small velvet bag. She tied the opening shut then sealed the string with wax and laid it aside to cool. She took a gold coin from the lining of her valise. It was the last one of the five she'd hidden there before leaving Paris. Then she placed both the velvet bag and the coin inside the bodice of her dress. When it became full light outside, she would find the trader from Charleston and ask him to send the letter to England. The gold coin should be more than enough to cover the cost.

Once the velvet bag was safely in the hands of the trader, she would deal with whatever was stalking her.

During the crossing from Europe to the island of

Jamaica, Count Cordelier and Andrea had been introduced to Madam Lorraine Devon. They were included in a private séance with the captain and several distinguished guests. The count was fascinated by the voodoo priestess's supposed ability to communicate with the souls of the dead. Andrea was temporarily caught up in the excitement of participating in the forbidden ceremony, but she quickly became disenchanted with the voodoo priestess.

Andrea looked forward to when the ship would dock in Kingston, Jamaica, and they would forever part company with Madam Devon. After three months at sea, finally, the island came into view and the passengers were notified they would be docking the next morning.

The weather had grown increasingly warm over the past month until it had become impossible to sleep because of the oppressive heat. The grain in the galley had become infested with weevils, and the water was tepid and tasted of the wooden kegs it had been stored in. There had been no fruit available for the crew for six weeks, and several members suffered from bleeding gums and other assorted maladies.

Finally, the ship was docked and the passengers began disembarking. Andrea was supervising the baggage handlers, while they loaded her trunks onto the carriage, when she saw several trunks she did not recognize. "Stop, stop," she called, aggravated at the delay. "Those trunks are not mine. They do not belong on this carriage."

"Sorry, Madam, but the gentleman instructed me to load these trunks onto this carriage."

"There must be some mistake," Andrea answered.

"Hold a minute while I clear it up." She walked across the yard and approached the count. "Darling," she said when he turned toward her, "there's some confusion with the trunks. Those men are loading someone else's baggage onto our carriage. I asked them to stop but they said they were following your instructions."

"They are following my instructions," he answered curtly. "We are accompanying Madam Devon to her home at Rose Hall for a few weeks' visit." He turned back to the captain, dismissing her.

Andrea stood rooted in place for a moment, considering his inconsiderate change of their plans and the possibility of spending days or weeks trapped in the voodoo priestess's company. Finally, she turned and walked back to where the men were loading the carriage. She climbed inside the carriage, leaving them to load the trunks however they wanted, unwillingly to face them since Reynaldo's rebuke. "How dare he?" She was filled with a cold dread for herself as well as for Reynaldo. "Oh well, it's only for a couple of weeks."

The trip across the mountain to Montego Bay, where Rose Hall Estate was located, was hot and difficult. The carriage became stuck in ruts, hidden by thick underbrush, several times and had to be pulled out before they could continue. The heat pressed down on them, making it hard to breathe. Inside the carriage Madam Devon and Count Cordelier talked, unconcerned about the heat. Andrea tried it ignore the conversation. They spoke of gems, traveling backward to other times, and eternal youth. Impossibly strange things that made Andrea cold with fear for Reynaldo and for herself. Finally, the conversation became too much for her. "So, Madam, is it true that Rose Hall was the home of Elizabeth Barrett

Browning?" she interrupted.

Both Reynaldo and Madam Devon looked toward her. "Please Andrea, Madam Devon and I are discussing business. Can you not amuse yourself for a while?" Reynaldo said curtly.

Madam Devon spoke quickly. "You are correct, Madam, Rose Hall was once owned by the Barrett family. As a matter of fact Elizabeth is buried there. It might also interest you to know she did most of her writing while she lived there. I've found several unpublished poems she left in an old chest of drawers. I'd be happy to show those to you if you're interested?"

Reynaldo was scowling at her, so Andrea was grateful for Madam Devon's quick thinking. Andrea looked into Reynaldo's angry face and then to Madam Devon.

"It's wonderful that you have an interest in Elizabeth Barrett Browning, Madam Baker," Madam Devon said. "Reynaldo, this is splendid. You were worried that Madam Baker would be bored while you and I concluded our business, but this will relieve you of that worry." She turned to Andrea. "There are many old books and journals for you to explore while you are at Rose Hall. I'm delighted to find another person who has an interest in that sort of thing." She touched Andrea's arm. Madam Devon's fingers were cold, reminding Andrea of the icy touch of a dead man. It caused her to shudder involuntarily.

After a few moments of uneasy silence, Madam Devon and Count Cordelier began talking again. This time Andrea listened silently. She decided it might be in her best interests to know what sort of business Reynaldo and Madam Devon were engaged in.

Andrea looked out the window, pretending to watch the scenery, while she listened. She could not help but notice the thick vines and trees overhanging the narrow road, threatening to close off the cleared space and trap the carriage in a mass of green.

Finally, the carriage emerged from the trees into a narrow lane through a seemingly endless field of sugar cane. After a while they saw the Rose Hall main house. An extremely large black man and a middle-aged black woman met them. Madam Devon instructed the woman to take Andrea and Reynaldo to a suite on the second floor of the estate. Andrea walked through the French doors onto the balcony. She was surprised to see that the balcony extended across the entire length of the house and overlooked the green sugar cane fields and, past them, the blue ocean. The endless blue water was broken by white crests as the waves beat against the shore.

Andrea was bone weary from the voyage, but the constant ocean breeze kept the heat at bay and lifted some of her weariness. Two other sets of French doors opened onto the balcony. She wondered who occupied those rooms. While she stood looking down the long balcony, Madam Devon stepped through the last set of doors. She walked to the balcony rail and turned toward Andrea. "The breeze is wonderful, is it not? The estate was built so that the breeze always blows across the balcony and in through the doors and windows. It makes no difference how hot the weather is outside, the rooms up here are always quite pleasant." She stood there another moment, looking at Andrea, then walked back inside.

When Andrea returned to her rooms, Reynaldo was gone. She looked at the trunks and moaned, dreading the prospect of unpacking and dealing with the clothes. She sighed heavily and pushed her sleeves up to her elbows.

She stopped when a light knock sounded on the door. Andrea opened it. "Good day, ma'am. Madam sent me to take care of your wardrobe." Andrea stepped aside gratefully. The girl was dark and slight, reaching Andrea's shoulder.

"Thank you so much." Andrea was relieved to have the job of dealing with the trunks out of her hands. "I'm afraid many of the clothes need cleaning and they all need airing. The conditions on the ship from France did not allow for proper care of them, and I fear some may be ruined."

"Yes, ma'am. I'll take care of whatever needs done." The girl didn't raise her eyes but Andrea got the impression they were fearful. Another knock sounded at the door. The girl moved quickly and gracefully to open it. "That'll be Mowhadon with your bath water. I guessed Madam would be wanting a bath as quickly as it could be arranged."

"Oh thank you," Andrea said. "A bath will be splendid." She sighed.

Silently as a cat, a large black man entered the room carrying two wooden buckets of water. Andrea recognized him as the same man who had greeted them when they first arrived.

He emptied both buckets into a large enamel tub in the adjoining room then left to bring more water. Andrea rushed back to where the girl was busy unpacking the trunks. "What a splendid surprise. I didn't know the tub was there. I'm so looking forward to soaking in the water and washing my hair."

The girl smiled shyly.

"What is your name?" Andrea asked.

"My name is Margaret but everyone calls me Magpie."

"Well, Magpie, I'm ever so grateful for your help. Thank you so much."

Magpie smiled and ducked her head, embarrassed to be hearing genuine thanks from a white woman.

Within a few moments the tall black man had filled the tub and was leaving the suite. "Thank you," Andrea said and he nodded to her.

"His name is Mowhadon." Magpie said. "He's the houseboy. He's strong as an ox but not exactly smart. Madam Devon likes having him inside the house. He's very loyal to Madam."

Andrea thought that was more explanation than had been expected but dismissed it as unimportant. "Can you manage a dress for me to wear to dinner this evening?" she asked.

"Yes ma'am, I'll make sure you have a nice clean frock to wear. I'll try to find one that will be cool. It gets awfully warm here. Madam doesn't serve dinner till nine, but even the late evenings are muggy. Does Madam need my help with her hair?"

"Could you? Oh, that would be splendid. I've not had anyone to help with my hair since I left France. If you could style my hair, I would be ever so grateful."

"Before I came to work for Madam Devon, I worked for a gentleman who operated a salon for the ladies who didn't have a personal maid to help with their grooming,"

Magpie said. "It'll be no trouble arranging your hair, ma'am."

Reynaldo left the suite upstairs and wandered down the winding stairs, through the parlor, and into the library. The walls of the room were dark mahogany with book-filled shelves from floor to ceiling along three sides. The fourth wall was windows and a door that opened onto a small porch.

The porch led into a garden filled with sweet-smelling flowers and lush green foliage. A rock walkway snaked through the garden. Reynaldo strolled around the garden noting that, here and there, the tall rock wall encircling the estate peeked through the greenery. The estate appears to be secure, he thought as he walked back to the library.

His eyes scanned the rows of books, each bound with a soft rich brown leather cover. Inside these volumes were the secret black arts Madam Devon practiced. He ran his hand along the books, reading each title. Finally, his hand rested on the book he'd been searching for: Destiny & Time. He wanted to take it off the shelf but suddenly felt an overwhelming fear. He quickly left the room, without taking the book, and returned to the garden.

Reynaldo was embarking on a dangerous journey with his and Andrea's lives at stake. He'd weighed the costs against the benefits before he'd made the decision to continue. He had considered talking to Andrea but decided against it. She would not understand. She would be revolted by the rituals, but she would be thankful once it was over.

"It's a beautiful place, don't you agree?" Madam Devon said.

Reynaldo jumped and turned in her direction. "Madam, you startled me," he answered curtly but then regained his composure. "Yes, it is beautiful. I was lost in thought and enjoying the evening smells."

"I'm sorry, I didn't mean to interrupt your thoughts. I thought you would be interested to know the preparations are proceeding on schedule, and everything is in place for the next moon passing."

"That is, indeed, welcome news, Madam. I'm most anxious to conclude this business. Andrea and I are anxious to continue on with our trip to America." He stepped away from the hand she had placed on his arm.

"Yes, I understand." She pretended not to notice his aversion to her touch. "Have you explained the ceremony to Madam Baker? It's important that she understand her part."

"When the time comes Andrea will be ready," he answered curtly. "Until that time I insist you do not involve her." He walked back to the open library door but stopped on the threshold.

"Madam, I trust nothing will go wrong and this business will be over quickly. I have paid you a great deal of money, and I will not tolerate delays or other adversities. Do we have an understanding?" He stood for another moment then continued into the house. Behind him Madam Devon smiled.

Over the next week Andrea wandered the estate grounds and walked along the beach, enjoying the warm sunshine and the beautiful island scenery. Several times she attempted to engage Reynaldo about her feelings, but he was sullen and withdrawn. She filled her time with books and poems from the estate library. True to her word, Madam Devon produced a large satchel filled with unpublished poems by Elizabeth Barrett Browning and several other authors.

Magpie was her only companion, but she proved to be an educated and articulate one. They were in the garden and Magpie was combing Andrea's hair. "Madam, how well do you know Madam Devon?" Magpie asked cautiously. "If you will pardon my saying, I cannot understand the connection. I would venture to guess Madam does not travel within the same circle of people you and the count travel. You are very different people."

For a moment Andrea considered her words. "You are correct, Magpie. We are quite different. I cannot imagine traveling in Madam Devon's circle of friends and, likewise, I do not believe that she would find my friends very interesting. I fear you think too highly of me though. I have often traversed a path filled with adversity. Most of which has been of my own making."

"How did you happen to be here, Madam?" Magpie asked.

"Reynaldo has some manner of business with Madam Devon. I do not presume to know or understand what that business involves. I only wish it was finished."

"Yes ma'am."

During the following week Reynaldo spent very little time inside the suite. Instead he was preoccupied with the library. Tonight the moon would enter the peak of what Madam Devon called the full-phase moon.

Tonight it would be the end of his and Andrea's life as they knew it, but it would be the beginning of life also. The new life for them both. "I trust you are prepared for tonight." Madam Devon stood behind Reynaldo, who was bent over reading a book he had borrowed from the library. He had read for hour after hour, over the past week, trying to still the feeling of dread that threatened to overcome him.

He answered without looking up. "What time will the ceremony begin? Is everything ready? Are you certain you have gathered all the necessary ingredients?" His heart pounded inside his chest as he contemplated what was to come. "We will be ready. I'm anxious to complete this and be on our way."

"As am I. I'll leave you to your reading." She reached across his shoulder to turn the book and look at the title. She smiled as she left the room. "Fool," she said under her breath.

Reynaldo could not calm his mind enough to concentrate on the words he had been reading. Finally, in frustration, he closed the book and returned to his room. Andrea was not there. He walked out onto the patio and scanned the beach, searching for her. He saw her walking with the dark-skinned girl she had befriended. Reynaldo wondered what the two could possibly have had to talk about for all those long hours they had spent together in the past week.

He considered the contrast between Andrea and Magpie. Andrea with her light brown hair, green eyes, and fair skin and Magpie with her dark curls along with eyes and skin to match. He felt a rush of tender feelings for Andrea and a no less intense rush of guilt for his treatment of her over the past month. Maybe I'll see about convincing Madam Devon to allow the girl Magpie to travel with us when we leave, he thought. That would please Andrea. I do not believe Madam Devon is very attached to her or anyone else, unless it is the big houseman she calls Mowhadon.

After an early dinner Reynaldo and Andrea retired to their room to await a summons from Madam Devon. "I don't relish the idea of wearing anything that woman owns," Andrea complained. "What difference can it possibly make which clothes I wear?"

"Don't be difficult." Reynaldo wrapped his arms around her and pulled her back against his chest. "I promise we will leave here tomorrow, and I'll have a surprise for you when we do. Now please put on the dress." He turned her around to face him and kissed her forehead. "Look, I'm wearing the things she sent." He pulled the robe away from his body and let it fall. "This is not precisely my idea of stylish attire but I'm not complaining now, am I?"

"Well, OK. I suppose I could go along this one time. You promise we will leave tomorrow?" She lowered her eyes.

"I promise. Now I'm going downstairs. I'll send Magpie up to help you dress." He kissed her lightly on the lips before leaving the room.

At exactly eleven o'clock a knock sounded at the door, and Reynaldo jerked himself to a standing position. Andrea had fallen asleep on the divan but awoke when the knock came. She rushed across the room to stand beside him. "I'm scared," she whispered.

He put his arm around her shoulders. "Don't be. Everything will be over tonight and we'll be on our way. Do you remember what I told you about the ceremony?" She nodded. "Good, now there is nothing to be afraid of."

Together they opened the door and followed the messenger out into the hall, down the winding stairs, and into the garden. The sweet smells from the flowers came immediately. Andrea found them strangely calming. The messenger led them through a gate in a wall that was hidden from view by a thick overgrowth of thorny vines.

Andrea held tightly to Reynaldo's arm as they walked down the pathway through the thick trees and vines. They followed the messenger for close to a mile. Finally, he stopped and motioned them forward. "Just beyond there you'll find a cave opening." He pointed to a bend in the path. "There'll be someone there to guide you." He stepped off the path and indicated that Reynaldo and Andrea should pass.

They went to the cave entrance and waited. After what seemed a very long time, a black-robed cleric stepped out of the cave and motioned for them to follow. Reynaldo placed Andrea's hand on his arm and squeezed it gently. They walked silently behind the figure down the narrow tunnel until the cave opened into a circular cavern about a hundred feet wide. In the center of the cavern, a large iron plate partially covered what appeared to be a round well opening. The plate was circular and measured some four feet across. A large stone chiseled to resemble a table extended over the edge of the well. All around the wall torches glowed, pushing back the darkness.

The black-robed guide led Reynaldo and Andrea to a stone bench across from the well. After a few tense moments, Madam Devon entered the cavern followed by twenty more black-robed clerics, walking in groups of five. The hems of their sleeves and the inside of their cowls were lined in silk, in a matching color. The cowls covered their faces. The loose-fitting robes made it impossible to determine the sex of the wearers. Madam Devon's robe was also black but otherwise bore no resemblance to the sexless ones worn by her followers. The silk shimmered and clung seductively to her body. The inside of her cowl shimmered gold and scarlet and hung down her back showcasing her hair, which she wore loose.

The twenty black-robed clerics formed a circle around the wall and stone table. Madam Devon walked to the iron plate then turned to face the circle of clerics. At her signal one of them stepped forward, removed a black velvet scarf from under the robe, opened it, and placed it on the flat surface of the iron plate.

Once the cleric was back in the circle, the madam motioned to another cleric, who stepped forward and produced a small black bag. This was placed in the center of the cloth.

The madam nodded to one cleric after another. Each one stepped forward, and they produced a small silver box, four silver candles, a silver pitcher, and four candles. Finally, the last cleric stepped forward and, from underneath the robe, pulled a curved, sheathed knife.

The silver-laced handle of the knife protruded from the black sheath. Andrea squeezed Reynaldo's arm and leaned against him. He patted her hand reassuringly. He wondered at the array of objects on the cloth-covered plate but fought to push his concerns aside. Think upon the reward. Once all of the clerics were back in the circle, they began to chant slowly and softly. Although Andrea could see their mouths moving, the sound was so soft it appeared to resonate from the walls of the cavern. Madam Devon lifted the flint from the silver box and struck it. It sparked immediately and appeared to jump from one candle to another until all four were burning brightly. She lifted the silver pitcher and poured clear liquid into the cups.

She carried the cups to Reynaldo and Andrea and handed them each one. She raised her cup in a salute. "This cup is symbolic of life. Drink in celebration and expectation of long life." Andrea and Reynaldo drank deeply, emptying their cups. Madam Devon returned the cups to the cloth-covered plate, and two clerics quickly gathered them up, along with the pitcher, and put them beneath their robes. Neither Reynaldo nor Andrea seemed to have noticed that Madam Devon drank only lightly. She opened the velvet bag and poured the contents onto the cloth-covered plate.

As the contents tumbled out of the bag, Andrea saw the gems glittering in the candlelight. Madam Devon picked up the first gemstone and held it high above the candles. It was an emerald, the largest one Andrea had ever seen. Madam Devon began to chant. Her voice held a sing-song quality. Andrea did not recognize the words. After a moment the chanting stopped and she said, loudly and clearly, "Emerald green stone of life." She placed the gemstone on one corner of the cloth. She picked up the next stone, held it high, and again began the chant.

"Opal the stone made to rule the water's depth." She placed the stone on another corner of the cloth, directly across from the emerald. Next she lifted the ruby and began the chant. "Ruby red the stone of blood." This stone she placed in the third corner. The last stone was crystal clear. "Diamond white to call forth the air."

After placing the diamond on the fourth corner, she turned to face Andrea and Reynaldo. "Come into the circle." She lifted her hands to motion them forward. Reynaldo rose eagerly but Andrea tried to pull him back. He put his arm protectively around her shoulders and raised her to her feet. Together they walked toward the opening. She felt more than saw the circle close behind her.

They walked to where Madam Devon stood waiting. She held out her hand. "The black diamond. I require the use of the black diamond from your ring."

Andrea's senses began to dull. Her vision blurred slightly. She did not want to give her ring to the voodoo priestess but felt unable to resist as Madam Devon pulled the ring from her finger.

Madam Devon had become completely immersed in her role as priestess. She lifted the ring high above her head and began to chant. "Keel el free Kata de fire para de fire para de inchor. Black diamond to join the elements. Black diamond to open the portal. Black as the heart of the depth. Reveal to me thy servant thy test."

From behind her Andrea felt more than heard drums begin to sound a slow, rhythmic beat. Suddenly fire leapt from the well opening. It moved, as if it were alive, along the rim of the well, flickering as if it were tasting each gemstone. The drums sounded louder and faster as Madam Devon began to sway back and forth.

Both Reynaldo and Andrea slumped to the floor. Reynaldo, even in his stupor, pulled her to him protectively. Four black men entered the cavern carrying aloft a young girl. The men were naked except for leather thongs made from some sort of reptilian skin. Each man was large and well-muscled. Their bodies glistened with oil and sweat.

The girl was also naked. The only covering she had was a wide silver torc around her slim waist. Her slim black body was stretched out on a platform, also made of reptilian skin, stretched taut across two long poles. Her eyes were open but stared blankly, neither recognizing nor comprehending the scene around her.

The circle of black-robed clerics opened, allowing them to enter. Two of the clerics left the circle to lift the girl onto the stone table. Tendrils of fire from the well reached out to touch the girl seductively as if caressing a lover's body. It nipped at her nipples and moved across her stomach. The girl screamed as the flame invaded her body.

Andrea's mind revolted, but she was unable to respond in any way. The stench of burning flesh filled the cavern. The girl screamed as the fire left the well and completely covered her body.

Madam Devon unfastened the clasp that held her robe together, and it slipped to the floor. She moved to the beat of the drums, her body now completely naked except for a silver belt and several strands of silver necklaces. As she moved she lifted the knife from its sheath and turned to sway above Andrea. From somewhere deep inside, a scream began to erupt from Reynaldo's body as he found the strength to pull himself up and between Andrea and the knife-wielding woman. "Nooooo!" He lunged toward the naked woman.

He managed to clasp her arms. As they grappled, the ring fell from her hand to land on the floor beside Andrea. She turned her head slowly to look where it lay then back to where Reynaldo wrestled with the naked voodoo priestess.

The black-robed clerics abandoned the circle to press forward in an effort to aid their mistress. From the circle one of the black-robed ones reached out and began lifting Andrea to her feet, pulling her from the melee. A dark-skinned hand plucked the ring from the floor and pushed it into Andrea's hand.

The cleric dragged Andrea from the cavern, forcing her drugged feet to walk. Andrea tried to reach Reynaldo, who had been forced down by the angry mob of black-robed followers of the voodoo priestess. The one rescuing her hissed, "It's no good. There's no help for him now. Hurry, we must save ourselves. We must get away quickly."

A flicker of recognition crossed Andrea's consciousness. She knew that voice.

Together they crossed the garden and entered the kitchen of Rose Hall Estate.

The black-robed cleric pulled a cloth sack from behind one of the cabinets along the wall and pushed it into Andrea's hands. As she did, the hood fell back, revealing Magpie's face. Magpie stuffed several loaves of bread and cheese into another bag then gripped Andrea's arm and pulled her through the door. "Come on. We must hurry. They'll soon be after us. We must be gone quickly." Andrea allowed herself to be pulled along the path away from the house and into the jungle. Later she could not recall much of the journey from Rose Hall.

She ate when Magpie pushed food into her hands and rested when Magpie told her to. At some point she and Magpie spent a night inside a rough cabin with other dark-skinned natives, who talked with Magpie in a strange sing-song language that Andrea did not recognize.

One of these men accompanied them when they left the cabin. He stayed with them all the way to the Kingston seaport. Once there, Magpie arranged passage for Andrea aboard a ship bound for New Orleans. Magpie stood on the dock and watched as the ship pulled away, carrying Andrea to America.

That was four months ago. Now, after Andrea had been in New Orleans for a month, Madam Devon's followers had found her.

JUDITH 1989

Chapter 2

I'm not exactly sure when I first realized Mama's ring was missing. I think the last time I saw it was last July. My sister Ida Mae and her family were visiting over the holiday. Every year on the Fourth, we take a picnic lunch to the park and spend the day. Our kids play in the water while the adults fish or ride the paddleboats. The holiday celebration always ends with a fireworks display put on by the rescue squad. This year they shot off the fireworks from a barge in the middle of the lake. By the time the fireworks were over, we'd been in the park a good ten hours and were sunburned and tired. The area by the lake was so crowded that my husband, Davis, and Ida Mae's Bill decided to go to the park early to stake out a good spot so we would be near the water to watch the kids swim.

Early in the day the park began to fill up with other families picnicking and playing in the water. Ice chests were filled with soft drinks or beer. Men and women of every shape and size imaginable strolled from one group to the next. Albert Lawson, with the artificial leg that he got after losing his real one to cancer, was teasing the children by pretending to fall and break his leg off, and Lisa Fielding was dressed to the hilt, wearing high heels and a hat and sporting a fresh flower corsage. At each stop the ice chests were opened and beverages offered. As the groups moved along the edge of the lake, they picked up additional members at some stops and lost some at other ones.

"Do you still have Mama's ring?" Ida Mae asked while we were spooning out potato salad and fried chicken for the second time that day. "I'd like to see it. Can we get it out later? I've been thinking about it a lot lately, and you know I can't ever remember seeing her wear it."

"I don't think I ever did either, come to think of it. Remind me when we get home and I'll get it out," I answered. Ida had never spoken openly about her resentment that Mama had left the ring to me instead of her, but I knew she felt it. The ring was the only piece in Mama's jewelry box worth more than a few dollars. I was sure the black stone was some sort of costume gemstone, but the ring was gold. As a matter of fact, the jewelry box itself was probably worth more than all the jewelry put together. It was made from mahogany and carved with flowers, leaves, and vines that trailed out to the edges of the lid and then down the corners of the box. The tiny vines wrapped around the edges of the panels covering the sides. The panels were carved from mother-of-pearl and changed from pinkish gray to pinkish blue depending on the light.

Mama's brother Paul gave her the box after he came back from the war in Italy. He had bought it, while on leave from the military, as a gift for his fiancé, Trula Blankenship. Uncle Paul was stationed in Milan, Italy, during the last days of the war. When he arrived back in Rockwood with the jewelry box in hand, he found Trula married to the local banker's son, Justin Williams, and pregnant with their first child.

Uncle Paul gave the jewelry box to Mama; then he bought a bus ticket and climbed aboard a Greyhound headed for San Francisco, California. He turned away from Rockwood and never returned, at least not while he was still alive. Paul was Mama's favorite brother, and she never got over him leaving Rockwood. She made a point of speaking kindly of Trula, but I always suspected she was hiding some really strong feelings. Then again, Mama never spoke unkindly about any living soul that I can remember. She believed in the golden rule and practiced what she preached.

Uncle Paul died two years before Mama. As a young man he'd had a couple of failed marriages, but for the last thirty years of his life he lived alone. Until the day Mama died, she believed Uncle Paul just never got over Trula Blankenship, and she treasured the jewelry box he'd given her.

The ring once belonged to Mama's maternal grandmother and was passed down to her oldest daughter, who passed it to mama, who passed it to me. I never understood why she gave the ring to me. I was neither the oldest nor the youngest. I fit exactly in the middle of the five girls in the family. By rights, I guess it should have gone to my oldest sister, Ida Mae.

On this particular Fourth of July, it was so late when we arrived back home from the festivities, we all slept late the next morning. I didn't come downstairs till nearly ten o'clock and was surprised to find Ida Mae sitting at the kitchen table going through Mama's jewelry box.

"Oh, hi, I was just looking at Mama's things and remembering how it was when she was still alive," Ida Mae stammered. "I didn't think you'd mind."

I stood speechless for a few seconds an angry retort on my lips. "No, not at all. Help yourself." I moved quickly to the coffee pot, hoping that having a cup of steaming coffee in my hands would help keep me from saying out loud what I was feeling. "Did you find the ring?" I asked when I finally felt confident of being able to control my voice.

"Yes I did. Oh, Judith, don't you ever wonder about the story behind this ring?" Ida Mae asked wistfully.

I looked at her across the top of my cup and shrugged. "I guess I've not got much of an imagination," I answered lamely, feeling a little guilty about being angry with her. Ida didn't mean any harm. After Mama's death she had become almost a second mother to me. She'd been there for me when Davis was diagnosed with cancer. Although it was found early and, after a year of chemo treatments, he was pronounced cancer free, the first months after his diagnosis were difficult for both of us. Ida was with me all the way.

Straggling soft curls framed her face, dimming the harsh look caused by her severe hairstyle. Her mouth held a small frown. Worry wrinkles creased her brow. I saw a quick flash of hurt cross her face then disappear. She seemed hesitant to speak at first but changed her mind. "I would so love to know about it. You know I've done a little research this past year, and I believe there's more to this ring than we've been told."

She talked excitedly now, trying to get my interest. "According to what I've found out so far, Great-Grandma Baker was not always the soft-spoken demure lady of the 1800s. Did you know she died in New Orleans, in 1880, under some pretty strange circumstances?" Ida

Mae whispered conspiratorially.

"What do you mean by strange circumstances?"

"Well, it seems that our dear great-grandmother left her boring working-class husband, along with two children, in England to travel Europe, the Caribbean Islands, then on to New Orleans with a somewhat less than reputable man by the name of Count Reynaldo Cordelie. And what's more, this count also traveled with a woman who was reported to have been some sort of voodoo priestess."

"Where'd you hear this stuff? It sounds like some dime-store novel. Come on, Ida Mae, you're talking about our great-grandmother here."

"I know! Listen, Judith, don't you think it's exciting? I mean someone in our ancestry was an adventuress."

"I don't believe a word of it," I snapped. "You're letting your imagination get the best of you. Are you finished looking at those?" I closed the lid of the box, without looking inside it, and returned it to the shelf where I'd kept it since Mama gave it to me six years earlier.

"Oh, Judith, look at us. We're boring. Just plain boring. Why, I'll bet you and Davis eat the same thing for breakfast every morning. I'll bet you go to the same restaurants, watch the same shows on TV, and I'll bet each of you knows exactly what the other will say before you say it. Don't you ever get tired of doing the same ole thing day in and day out? Look, Judith, I've been researching Great-Grandmother Baker's life, and I really envy her. She saw what she wanted and went after it. She gave up everything to be with the man she loved. I think it's romantic and beautiful."

I shook my head in disbelief. "Get a life, Ida. I can't believe you're idolizing a woman who deserted her family. If what you say about her is true, then she left her husband and kids to run with this count and his voodoo priestess friend. She was an adulteress, for God's sake. If she died while still in his company, I say good riddance."

Ida Mae looked at me as if I'd slapped her face. "Judith, don't be so judgmental. You forget everybody's life is not as easy as yours," she snapped. She left the kitchen. I heard the front door close and, when I pulled back the curtain, I watched her stuff her hands into the front pockets of her faded jean shorts as she walked past the edge of the driveway and onto the sidewalk toward town.

"Why did I do that?" I immediately wished I'd been more understanding and was sorry for making her angry. I poured my coffee into a to-go cup and headed out the door to catch her and apologize. Ida Mae didn't need any problems from me. She had enough trouble in her life. Bill had been laid off from the job he'd held for twenty-five years, and his luck with finding a new one was not encouraging. Bill worked as a mechanic for a large apparel company that had moved its operations offshore earlier in the year. He was one of many casualties. He'd refused the state's offer to go back to school and learn a new profession. He was too old to start over, or so he said, and after not finding a job quickly he'd given up and quit looking, choosing to work around the house, sulk, and curse his former employer and everyone who still had a job. Ida Mae took a job in a real estate office to pay the bills.

She didn't need me putting her down. I'll apologize and encourage her to explore the ring's origin, I decided while chasing her down the street. Even though things were good for Davis and me now, it had not always been that way. There was a time, just after he got out of the Navy, that we'd gone through some pretty rough times.

CALIFORNIA
Chapter 3

As I rushed down the street after Ida Mae, I remembered the time when Davis and I were first married. He was just out of the Navy and I was pregnant with our first baby.

We were in California, living near the Naval Base in San Diego, and we both really liked it there. The weather was always so nice and, when Davis was home, we could walk along the beach. We both loved the beach early in the morning. We carried our shoes while we walked along the long stretches of warm sand. The water rushed in and covered our feet then receded. We watched the tiny sand crabs hurry to bury themselves in the sand.

When Davis left the Navy we decided to stay in California. I suppose it was me more than Davis who wanted to stay. He wanted to go back home to Tennessee, but I was in love with the ocean and carefree living in the California sunshine.

Davis found a job with one of the small companies located in what is now called the Silicon Valley. Back then it was just a small area with a half dozen new high-tech companies struggling to build on a dream. He was working in the maintenance department of a company called Nu Tech. He cleaned and maintained the equipment used by the technicians who held tight to the dream of fast travel and fast communications for the world.

Davis worked a twelve-hour shift for ten days; then he was off for three days. The money wasn't bad and we were able to put back almost half of every paycheck. We were saving to buy a home. My dream was to live where I could see the ocean. Davis's dream was to buy a farm back in Tennessee. In the meantime we lived in a small apartment near San Jose.

Davis was seldom home and, even when he was there, he was always dead tired and spent the days collapsed in his chair in front of the TV. I was never able to stroll along the beach and experience my beloved ocean anymore. I was trapped inside the small apartment. To make things worse his work shift was changed to evenings. This meant he left home at 2:00 p.m. and got back at 2:00 a.m. I was in bed when he got home, and by the time I got up in the morning he was usually ready to go to sleep. I tried to be quiet so I didn't disturb him, but I soon became stressed.

Davis installed a viewing hole in the door so I could see who was there before I opened it. He never left the apartment without cautioning me to keep the door locked. This was not at all the life I had imagined, and I was beginning to hate the apartment. I had not seen the ocean since moving here. The strain was beginning to take its toll on me, and I began to hate the fact that I was pregnant. I finally decided to make a change. I packed a bag lunch and set out to walk into town. I left Davis a note in case he woke up before I returned, but I had no intention of being gone that long. I knew he'd have a fit about me going out alone.

I wasn't going anyplace in particular. I just needed

to be outside. I walked the mile into town and began exploring the side streets. I'd been to the grocery store with Davis, but it was located outside the main part of town in a new shopping center. Today I was seeing a whole new side of things. I guess the high-tech companies were attracting the best technical minds from around the world, causing the downtown area to develop in a new direction. The streets in the old part of town were bricked, not paved and small specialty shops along the streets catered to people who had moved there from around the world. There were shops that catered to the Chinese, the Swiss, the English, the Austrians and even some Germans. There was even a small shop that sold only American goods—I guess it was there for foreigners. I loved browsing through each of them. All this diversity was like a drug to my senses.

Here, within walking distance of my cramped apartment, was all this. Growing up in Rockwood, Tennessee, I never expected to see much more of the world than maybe Nashville or Atlanta. The trip with Davis to California had been the most exciting thing in my life until that day.

On my first visit into town, I just walked along the streets and looked through the shop windows. I was so intrigued by the sights and smells that I totally forgot the time. I barely made it home before Davis got out of bed.

The next day I headed back into town as soon as I was sure he was sound asleep. I left a note saying I was going for a walk just in case he woke up and looked for me. I began buying little things from the shops. They were small but not necessarily inexpensive. I knew I'd never travel to places like London or Paris, but I wanted to say I owned things like a vase from Paris or a picture from Amsterdam. Whenever I got back to our tiny apartment, I hid whatever I had purchased so that I would not have to tell Davis about my trips into town alone.

I met Ingrid Hanson late one Tuesday evening in early July. I stayed at home that day until Davis left for work. I was six months pregnant and it seemed like I always needed to sit down and rest. That day I was sitting on the bench in what passed for a town square. It was really just an area with wooden benches surrounded by a dozen older shops. The shop owners had made the park area years earlier, before high-tech company employees invaded the small town bringing fast food shops and foreign-owned markets. Ingrid was my first real friend in California.

"Hi, my name is Ingrid." She plopped down on the bench beside me. "I've noticed you visiting our shop several times. Have you ever tried the apple turnover we sell?" She acted as if she had known me all of her life. "My aunt Kotti makes it fresh every morning."

"Oh, hi," I answered a little shyly. "No I haven't tried it, but it does smell wonderful. I wasn't sure what I should eat with the baby and all." I pointed to my round belly. I usually bring a sandwich from home."

"Well, there's nothing any better than Aunt Kotti's turnovers for you and the baby. You just wait right here." Ingrid jumped up from the bench, headed across the square, and disappeared into the tiny German bakery. She emerged a few seconds later and ran back across the square carrying something wrapped inside a cloth napkin. Before she reached the bench where I was waiting, I smelled the apples and spices.

Ingrid handed the napkin to me. "There now, you

just bite into that and you'll think you've died and gone to heaven."

I accepted the gift and opened the napkin. I breathed in the smell of fresh apples and cinnamon. "It smells wonderful." I hesitated only a few seconds before shoving my bologna sandwich back into the bag and stuffing it into the space between us on the bench.

"Well, don't just sit there smelling, eat it," Ingrid said.

Over the next hour we talked of growing up. We talked of family and husbands and children to come. By the time I noticed the time, the sun's rays were sliding over the horizon. "Oh my goodness. Look at the time. I need to go. I don't like the idea of walking home after dark," I said anxiously, looking around.

"Where do you live?" Ingrid asked.

"Just outside of town about a mile or so. My husband and I live in the Woodland apartment building."

"Wait here. I'll get my bike and walk with you." Ingrid ran back across the square and into the alleyway beside her aunt's shop. She emerged pushing a bicycle and waved me over. "I'll push the bike and walk with you, and then I can ride back."

Over the next two weeks, we became fast friends.

"However do you Americans stand to have everything you buy wrapped up in that mountain of plastic?" Ingrid asked one day. "I went to the grocery for Aunt Kotti this morning and, I tell you, I couldn't tell what I was buying. I couldn't smell to see if the fish was fresh and, to tell you the truth, I heard on the news that some of the stores are putting formaldehyde into the meat to keep it from turning. There could have been some in the fish I bought. I sure couldn't smell it with all that plastic around it." Ingrid frowned. Then she smiled and changed the subject. "I don't think you need to be walking this distance every day. My aunt Kotti said to tell you to stay home and I will bring your apple turnover to you. She says you are going to be having the baby within the month. What do you say? Aunt Kotti is always right."

"Well, I'll admit it is becoming a task to get here," I confessed, "but your aunt is wrong about the time. I have another six weeks to go." As we walked I suddenly remembered the earlier conversation. "Do you mean they don't wrap the food in Germany?" I asked. "How do they keep the flies off?"

"Flies? What flies? Don't you know America is the only country in the world with flies?" Ingrid teased.

"No! You don't mean it?"

"Sure I do. It's God's curse on you, didn't you know? God is a Jew after all." Ingrid's expression was serious.

"Well, sure he is, but what makes you think God hates Americans?" I answered indignantly, not really knowing if God was a Jew or not. "What right does he have to hate us? We've never done anything against him."

Ingrid began to laugh at my naive belief. "I'm just teasing you. Of course we have flies. We just swat them off the meat and go on."

Over the next two weeks, Ingrid made the trip every morning to deliver the fresh turnover to me. During this time she first got to know Davis.

"What is that smell?" Davis came into the kitchen

where Ingrid and I sat at the table wolfing down the bag of apple turnovers that Ingrid's aunt had sent. "Whatever it is I hope you saved some for me."

"Oh, hi honey." I was embarrassed to be caught enjoying the company of someone I had not told Davis about. "Davis, this is my friend Ingrid Hanson and these are apple turnovers from her aunt's bakery. Come on in and help us. There's more than we need."

If Davis thought there was anything unusual about the situation, he didn't let on. "Hello, Ingrid. I'm Davis, and if you have the keys to the bakery that made these, then we are destined to become friends." Davis pulled out a chair and took a turnover from the bag. I gradually began to relax as the conversation between my husband and my friend continued for the next hour.

Finally, Davis stood up. "I hate to leave good company but I have to get a shower. I'm taking an early shift today and I have to be there by noon. Ingrid, it's good to finally get to meet one of Judith's friends. I see she's in good hands." He kissed the top of my head and left to get ready for work.

Two weeks later on February 12, 1960, Martha Leah Barnes was born. She had wispy blonde hair and fair skin. It was not possible to tell the color of her eyes because all babies have gray eyes when they're born, but this didn't stop Davis and me from arguing over their color. Ingrid swore that she could see blue coming into them every day, while Davis maintained they were green like his mama's.

Davis and I were both in awe of the tiny, perfect creature we had caused to come into the world. Davis silently vowed that his daughter would never go through the hardships he and his brothers and sisters had seen while growing up in Lancing, Tennessee.

Ingrid brought flowers and balloons and filled the tiny hospital room with noise and excitement. She stood outside the nursery window with Davis and me and beamed as if she had been a part of the event.

We brought Martha home to the small apartment, where we had prepared a room decorated with Winnie the Pooh curtains and cut-outs hanging on the walls. When we arrived at home, we found a large box on the porch. It was wrapped in silver paper with pink bunnies, and it was tied with a big pink bow. "Who could it be from?" I asked after Davis had pulled it into the living room.

"I don't know. There's no card. Here, I'll take the baby while you open it."

I untied the ribbon and pulled the paper from the box. "It's a stroller! It's a stroller! Here, a card. Let's see. It's from your family. Can you believe it?"

"Here's the card. 'Thank your friend Ingrid for helping us with the surprise. Congratulations. Mama and Daddy.' It's signed Faye, Arthur, Mama, and all the family."

Davis smiled. "I can take Martha on long walks. She and I can go into town. This is great."

Davis returned to work the next afternoon, leaving us at home. After a week I decided I was well enough to make the walk into town, and I called Ingrid. "Don't come out. Martha and I are coming to town. Roll out the red carpet."

As I dressed and prepared Martha for her first trip

away from the apartment, the doorbell rang. Davis had installed the viewer and cautioned me daily about always looking through it before opening the door, but today I was happy with all the world and it slipped my mind. The two men standing on the stoop wore ski masks. They shoved me back into the room and closed the door. The taller of the two men pulled a knife from inside his coveralls. "Don't make a sound and we won't hurt you."

The tall man shoved me onto the couch. "What do you want! I don't have any money." I pulled myself to my feet and ran toward the stroller where baby Martha slept. "Please, I don't have any money. You've come to the wrong house." The heavyset man grabbed me from behind and covered my face with a foul-smelling rag. The odor was suffocating me. I struggled to pull free of the man's grasp. I felt myself losing consciousness. My last thought was for my baby, and then the darkness took me.

Ingrid walked to the door and looked down the street. When Judith had called earlier, she'd said she and the baby were ready to leave for town. That was over an hour ago. "They should be here by now," she said to Aunt Kotti for the third time. She stepped out onto the sidewalk and looked in the direction she knew Judith would be coming from. She walked a few feet down the street. After pacing back and forth for a few minutes, she went around the side of the building and retrieved her bicycle. "I'm going to ride out a ways, Aunt Kotti. Maybe she's having trouble pushing the stroller."

Ingrid rode her bicycle down the narrow paved road leading from the main part of town to the Woodland apartments. By the time she reached the apartment where Judith and Davis lived, she was beginning to get really worried. I'm probably being silly, she thought, but her feet pedaled faster and faster as she neared the building.

When she finally arrived, she banged loudly on the door. "Judith!" she yelled. "Open the door." She reached for the doorknob expecting to find it locked, but it turned easily and Ingrid pushed the door open. "Judith, Judith are you OK?" she yelled." Judith!"

Judith lay on the floor between the couch and the doorway. Oh, my God, Judith!" She lifted her friend's head onto her lap. She smelled a strange odor on the rag lying on the floor beside her friend. "Judith, wake up!" she pleaded. Slowly Judith began to move her head.

My first thought was of my baby.

"Martha. Where's Martha?" I struggled to rise.

"Lie still. I'll get her," Ingrid promised. "What happened to you? Did you faint? What in the world in that smell?" She went into the nursery and came back into the living room. Ingrid looked into the stroller and then at me. I began to scream.

"Martha! Where's my baby? Oh God, they took my baby!"

Ingrid ran to where I stood gripping the edge of the couch.

"They took my baby." I sobbed.

By the time the police arrived, I was past crying. I sat with my arms wrapped around my body, rocking back and forth. Ingrid repeated the story that I had told her. I listened, not believing the words could be true.

"Mrs. Barnes," the detective asked, "try to think. Can you tell me anything more about the two men? Are you positive you've never seen either of them before?"

I began to cry again. "No, no, I told you they both wore ski masks pulled over their faces."

Davis and I spent the next five days alternating between disbelief and anger. Davis had not attended church since he left home for the Navy four years earlier, but he believed in God and knew Jesus had died for all of us. So, like most people in times of crisis, he prayed.

The FBI agent assigned to the case knew, with almost certainty, that the baby had not been taken for ransom, but he still tapped the phone and posted an agent in the house for the first two days.

Ingrid brought enough clothes to stay for several days. She slept on a fold-out cot in baby Martha's room. For a week she pleaded and cajoled Davis and me into eating and sleeping.

"I just don't understand," Davis asked the agent assigned to stay with us. "Why take our child? We have no money, our families have no money, we don't even know anyone with money."

"We're not sure. To be perfectly honest, in most cases like this, the kidnappers are in the baby-selling business. We have a pretty reliable source telling us that this is the case here." "Why our baby? Why Martha? Good grief, man, she's only been in this world ten days." Davis demanded. I could imagine what he was thinking. God, you could have prevented this. Why did you let this happen?

The agent answered grimly, "These people come into an area and stake out the local doctors' offices to watch for pregnant women. They usually have a profile of what the parents should look like. You see, the people they work for want the child to resemble the prospective parents as much as possible. Once they find a woman with the right physical appearance, they will follow her until they get a look at the father. Once they have determined that both the father and the mother meet the criteria that have been given to them, they stake out the woman and watch for the child to be born."

"Just tell me the truth," Davis pleaded. "What are the chances you'll be able to find her?"

Agent Kelly just shook his head in reply.

Finally, after ten miserable days and no break in the case, Agent Kelly was sent to tell us that, even though the FBI would continue searching, the agent and the phone tap were being removed from our home.

Ingrid went home the next day. "I'm sorry Davis," she explained. "I have to get back to the shop. My aunt has been working twelve hours a day for the last two weeks, and she's just too old to keep it up. She needs me at the shop. Uncle Frank and Aunt Kotti took in my brother Hans and me after our parents were killed. I'm really sorry. I'll be out after work. I promise."

"I understand," Davis answered. "You have to get on with your life and so do we. I appreciate everything you've done. We're not giving up hope, Ingrid." He shoved his fist into the door jam. "We're not giving up."

Ingrid biked the mile into town, the road blurred by the tears that filled her eyes. Her heart was breaking for her friends. She arrived home in time to let her aunt know she would open the shop and allow her aunt a few hours of needed sleep.

Each day Ingrid worked from eight in the morning till six at night; then she hurried to her bicycle and pedaled a mile to check on Judith. Each day she found her friend had slipped deeper and deeper into hopelessness. "Come into town tomorrow and visit with me at the shop. Aunt Kotti asks about you every day. She'd be so glad to see you." Ingrid begged.

Davis had gone back to work. Judith understood that he had no choice. The rent still came due just as it had before Martha was taken away. As often as Ingrid begged Judith to come into town, she refused. "I need to be here in case the police call."

A month has passed and still there has been no word. I don't believe we'll ever see baby Martha again, Ingrid worried as she carried the box of beeswax candles from the storeroom in the back of the shop. Uncle Frank had installed new shelving for the candles and other newly imported craft items he planned to offer for sale. Ingrid's mind was not on her work. She worried constantly about Judith and wondered about the baby's whereabouts. The police believed the child was being well cared for. Ingrid prayed they were right. "Lord," she prayed for the thousandth time, "please keep her safe."

The bell over the front door jingled. "Hey Hans. You here?" A voice called out. Ingrid started to get up from the floor, where she sat arranging the candles. "Hans, man, where are you?" The voice called again.

Ingrid heard her brother come in from the storeroom. "Hey Stan. What's up?"

"Are you ready to make some real money, Hans my man?"

Ingrid recognized the voice as belonging to Stanley Lewis, one of her brother's new friends.

"What you got in mind?" Hans asked. Ingrid pressed her body back into the corner and tried to stay quiet.

"We have another request from Mr. K. He was real happy with our last delivery, so he's sent another order."

"I don't know, man," Hans answered uneasily.

"What'd you mean you don't know? You said you wanted to make some real money. Do you want to or not?" Stan demanded.

"Well, yeah, I do but, it's just, I don't know if I want to do something like that again."

"Look, this is easy money and nobody gets hurt. That kid, it'll be better off. Don't you know those people who got the kid have to be rich to pay the kind of money we're talkin' about?"

"Yeah, well, I know but still I don't think I want to do that again," Hans said.

"Look we've got an order and we've got a target over in the valley. She's about ready to drop it. If you change your mind, let me know. I need to call J. B. to help if you don't have the guts." Stan left the shop.

When Ingrid heard the bell, she started to rise and confront her brother but thought better of it and remained silent. She listened as her brother went back into the storeroom and released the breath she had been holding. As soon as she knew the room was empty, she ran to find the card that Agent Kelly had given her with his phone number. Ingrid's hands trembled as she dialed the number.

In the weeks following baby Martha's return, Davis and Judith decided to return home to Tennessee.

"I wish you would change your mind and stay." Ingrid was helping Judith wrap the dishes in newspaper and pack them for the trip back to Tennessee.

"We can't. This just is not our kind of place, and the people here are just not our kind of people," Davis said. He turned to their only real friend in California and took her hands. "You've been a good friend and we'll miss you, especially Judith, but we're going home. I've saved a little money and we're going back to where our baby girl can play outside in the yard and be safe."

The information Ingrid had given the FBI had provided the lead they needed to find Martha and break up a major baby-selling ring operating in California, Nevada, and New Mexico. Martha was back home along with five other babies, some of whom had been missing for as much as a year and a half.

Once Martha was safely home, Davis called a friend whose father owned a trucking company in Memphis, Tennessee. He'd been trying to get Davis to come to work with him since their time together in the Navy. Davis gratefully accepted the job offer, and he and Judith began getting things packed and ready to go.

The job would not start for a month, so they would have plenty of time to visit both families and find a house. When Davis heard that he would be working out of the Knoxville office, he was elated because he and Judith would be able to spend time with their families again.

He hoped to be able to help out with some money for his mama, who was still raising six of his thirteen brothers and sisters. His sister Faye and her husband Arthur helped his mama; he knew that. He wondered what would happen to them without that help. Years of drinking had made his paw a near-invalid, and the family existed mostly on what they grew in the garden.

Davis thought about the money he and Judith had saved to buy a house, and he felt selfish and guilty. I'll see what they need and try to take care of it, he thought for the thousandth time.

Davis's mama was a great believer in God and his willingness to take care of his children's needs, so even when things got to be pretty bad she always felt they would turn out for the best in God's own time.

Davis believed in God too, but he had long since decided it was best to take the care of his family's fate in his own capable hands. It wasn't that he doubted God's ability; he had serious reservations about believing God was inclined to involve himself in his day-to-day problems. "You know there'll be no sleeping late on Sunday morning when we get back home don't you, Judith?" he said while driving the rented moving van across Arkansas, and Judith laughed.

"I know your mama. She's like mine when it comes to church attendance. We should have been going to church all along, Davis. I miss church and Mama would have a fit if she knew we weren't going every week."

MAMA BARNES
Chapter 4

Althea Barnes hurried to change the sheets on Faith's small bed. Being the oldest of Althea's six children still living at home, Faith was the only one with her own room. Faith's not gonna like sharing Kathryn and Alma's room while Davis and his family are here, but she'll just have to get used to it, Althea thought. Faith will do what she's told. She always does.

Davis had not been home to Lancing since before he and Judith married two years earlier, and Althea was so looking forward to having them with her for a few days. And there was baby Martha. When Althea's grandchild had been kidnapped, she had been beside herself with worry. That was another the reason this visit meant so much to her. Althea wouldn't feel like the ordeal was really over until she could actually hold the child in her arms.

Of course Davis and his family would only be staying a few days, just until they found a house. Althea looked forward to keeping baby Martha while Davis and Judith searched for a place to rent. Usually Althea could allow her children and grandchildren to come and go, entrusting them to God's care, but since the kidnapping she'd had an overwhelming need to have the baby close by.

When she heard the engine of Davis's truck as

he pulled up in front of the house, she pulled back the thin curtain and looked out the bedroom window. She brushed back the wisps of hair that had escaped from her bun and rushed to the door to greet her oldest son.

"Hello, Mama," Davis said shyly as she pulled him down to hug him. Althea stood five feet in her shoes while her son was a good six feet tall.

"I'm so glad you're finally here, son. Where's Judith and the baby?" Althea strained to see into the cab of the truck.

"We're here, Mama Barnes." Judith came around from the back of the truck bed.

Althea left her son and hurried to greet Judith. She hugged her close but then quickly reached for the baby. "Here, let me have her. Oh my, just look at her." Althea hugged her granddaughter close. "You come on in here with your grandma. I've got everything ready for you. I've been waiting for you," she gushed. "Come on in, kids. I've got your supper on the stove."

Davis and Judith followed his her into the kitchen. "Something sure smells good, Mama," Davis said, breathing in the kitchen smells.

"Oh, it's just fried chicken and mashed potatoes. I remember it's your favorite meal. You know where the plates are."

"Biscuits. Look here, Judith. It's homemade biscuits." Davis pulled back the towel that covered the basket of bread.

Althea sat down in one of the metal kitchen chairs and began rocking back and forth, singing softly to the near-sleeping child.

I sing because I'm happy. I sing because I'm free.

His eye is on the sparrow and I know he watches me.

His eye is on the sparrow and I know he watches me.

Hearing his mama sing took Davis back in time to his childhood, when the sound of his mama's voice lulled him to sleep every night. He backed up against the stove, nibbled on a warm biscuit, and listened.

I'll put her down on the bed in the room I fixed for you. Why don't you get your bags so you don't wake her up later?" Althea suggested when she saw the baby was sleeping soundly. She had held her the whole time Davis and Judith ate the food she had made.

Davis looked sheepishly toward his wife Judith for help, but he saw none was forthcoming. "Mama, wait a minute," he said. "We're, uh, we're not staying. We're staying over at Faye's."

Althea didn't answer. The disappointed look on her face said it all.

"Mama, it's just that Faye's got those extra rooms so we won't be putting anybody out." When his mother still didn't answer, he added, "Well it's just better for us." He knew nothing he said would change the hurt look in his mama's eyes, so he turned back to his meal.

"I understand," Althea said. "Faye has a lot of room, that's for sure." She turned to leave. "I'll just lay the baby down till you're ready to leave."

Once she had left the room, Judith turned on her husband. "How could you do that? We should be staying here. You have no business hurting your mama's feelings."

"No, Judith. I told you I'm not staying here. Now be quiet before Mama hears you arguing," Davis snapped.

The next half hour passed uncomfortably. No one seemed to have much to say.

"It's been a long day for us, Mama. We'd better get on over to Faye's. I've drove nine hours today and I'm beat," Davis explained.

Althea did her best to cover her disappointment as she walked outside to the truck with her son and his family.

"We'll be busy looking for a house tomorrow so I don't expect we'll be back over," Davis explained. "Why don't you and Paw brings the kids over to Faye's tomorrow night for supper. Then we could all visit." He climbed into the truck's cab. "You know Faye won't mind."

Althea smiled. "We'll see. You all be careful now. Don't take any chances. You've come a long way to have an accident happen now."

Before Davis started up the truck's engine, he turned back to where his mama stood waiting, her arms wrapped around herself as if in a hug. "Mama. I didn't even ask about Paw and the other kids. Where are they?"

"Why Davis, this is Wednesday night prayer meeting. The kids are there at the church and your paw took the car over to pick them up so's they don't have to walk back in the dark."

Davis knew his mama never missed Wednesday prayer meeting, and he felt guilty that she had stayed at home to be there to greet him and his family when they arrived. "Well tell 'um all I said hi and try an' get everybody over to Faye's tomorrow. OK, Mama?"

Davis turned the key and the truck engine roared loudly, drowning out his wife's words. Judith tugged at Davis's sleeve. "I said! Don't do this. Don't leave your mama feeling bad like this. Can't you see she's upset? She went to a lot of trouble to fix us a place to stay." Davis didn't answer so she pulled his sleeve again. "Davis, your mama never misses church."

An hour later Althea's children returned from church expecting to see their big brother and his family. Instead they found their mama crying. This was something none of them could ever remember seeing before.

Sometime during the next three weeks, Davis found a house twenty miles from Piney and fifteen miles from Judith's mama in Rockwood. He was close enough to Knoxville that he could easily make the drive to work every day. He considered himself lucky to have found it. The house had five acres, a barn, and a chicken coop. Davis looked forward to finally being able to have a few farm animals to tend to after work. All was well in his life again. He didn't know the storm his return had started brewing among his brothers and sisters.

The story about his mama's hurt feelings spread quickly among the sisters and brothers and their wives and husbands. Even though some of the adults took care to keep their talking out of earshot of the children, others were not so careful and the story soon made its way from one cousin to the other.

"I don't know why Faye and Loretta are standing up for Davis after the way he acted," Davis' sister Gladys said. She and Jewel, another sister, were making Halloween costumes for her three children and Jewel's five.

"I think he's outgrown his raising," Jewel answered hotly. "I don't know if it's him or Judith."

"I don't think it's Judith. She always seems like a sweet person. She don't act like she thinks she's better than Mama. No, I think it's Davis. He thinks now that he's been in the Navy and now that he's got that fancy job where he wears a suit to work, he's too good to stay in Mama's house."

"I talked to Gerald today," Gladys said. "He's going to have it out with Davis."

"What did you say? When is he going over to Davis's house?" Jewel asked.

"I don't know but Gerald said he's going to catch him before Sunday and church. He said he wasn't going to put up with them coming back here like they was big shots and treating Mama like that."

"Well, I've always thought Davis and Faye both thought they were better than the rest of us, and Loretta ain't much better," Jewel declared.

"Loretta? I've never noticed Loretta being anything but plain ole Loretta, but I agree about Davis and Faye."

"When's the last time Loretta was in your house? I'll bet it was before she bought that beauty shop of hers."

"Well, yeah, I guess you're right," Gladys answered. "But I see her at church sometimes."

"Yeah, you see her and that friend of hers, Millie what's-her-name, but you don't see her going to Mama's and you don't see her coming over here, now do you?" Jewel was caught up in her own anger. "She goes to Faye's house though, now don't she?"

"Yeah, come to think of it I guess you're right," Gladys agreed.

"If you ask me Loretta has become a little snooty ever since she got her own beauty shop."

Gladys nodded in agreement but, just then, their kids ran into the house, so the sisters stopped their conversation.

DAVIS
Chapter 5

Davis and Judith arrived at his sister Faye's home on Wednesday night, sometime around 8:30. They went to bed early, claiming exhaustion, so Faye had very little time to talk with them. Over the next few days, he and Faye fell back into the easy camaraderie they had shared as children. Even so it surprised Faye when, soon after arriving from California, he told her his feelings about their parents. "We're not going to stay with Mama and Paw next week if it's all right with you that we stay here."

Faye looked at Davis, who was sipping on a cup of coffee, while she cooked breakfast. "Well, Davis, it's OK with me, but I think you'll find Mama will have something to say about it. Why don't you want to stay there? I know they don't have much room, but if you want I can bring some of the kids over here to make room for you."

"It's not the room. I don't want Judith and Martha exposed to the way things are there."

"The way things are there? What does that mean? The crowded rooms? The ragged furniture? The condition of the house? Paw?"

"You know what I mean, sis. It's the whole thing. I don't want them around Paw when he's drinking and, yeah, I know he's sober right now but it's more than that.

I know Mama is going to start on us about church and forgiving those men who took Martha and well, Faye, I just don't want to hear it."

Faye stopped stirring the gravy, pushed the skillet off the stove eye, and sat beside her brother. "When's the last time you and Judith went to church?" she asked.

"What's my going to church got to do with it? If I'd been going to church, do you suppose for one minute that it would have stopped those men from taking my baby? You sound just like Mama. Always connecting everything to religion."

Faye smiled and ruffled Davis's hair as if he were still a boy. "Don't tell me you've forgotten what Mama taught us? Everything in life is connected. God connected everything in our lives and he has control of all of it."

"Oh, come on, Faye. I've been through a lot. First with the war and then with almost losing the baby. I'm not sure I believe that anyone has control."

Faye refilled Davis's cup and sat down beside him again. "Yes, you have brother. You've seen more trouble than most of us will ever see, but God did take care of it now, didn't he? We all prayed for the baby's safe return just like we prayed for yours when you were on that ship out in the ocean." She touched his arm. "God will always care for his children if you allow him to. You have to do your part though, Davis. He won't force his will on any of us."

"OK, OK, I'll give you that I guess," Davis replied. "Judith and I both prayed hard when Martha was missing, and I know you and Mama did too. I guess I'm just hating to face Mama with the fact that I've changed since I left home and I've not been to church since I left for the

Navy," Davis finished lamely. "Another thing, I don't and I won't forgive the men who took my baby. I don't want Mama to start with that." Davis abruptly stood and left the kitchen.

Over the next month the story of how Davis had hurt Mama's feelings caused a flurry of phone calls and visits among his sisters and brothers. Not only did those living close by hear the story, so did Stephen and William, who lived in other states. Between Halloween and Thanksgiving, the telling and retelling of events reached a fever pitch.

It had all begun when Gladys and Jewel arrived at their mama's house, with four of their eight children in tow, to visit Davis and his family. They were anxious to see that the baby was OK after her ordeal and see Judith. Both Gladys and Jewel were prone to gossiping, so the thought of hearing firsthand, from Judith, about baby Martha's kidnapping and subsequent return was inviting.

They arrived only to find that Davis had taken his family to stay with their sister Faye instead of staying at their mama's house.

"Faye has two empty bedrooms, so it just made sense for them to stay there," their mama explained. "It's better for the baby, too. She won't have to sleep in the room with them."

Gladys spoke up. "I'm surprised that Judith will allow the baby out of her sight after what happened. Mama, did you tell them you had fixed a room for them here?"

Jewel noticed her sister Faith standing just inside the door to the kitchen, listening. She looked at her and frowned. Faith motioned to her that she wanted to talk. "I'm going to the little girls' room. I'll be right back," Jewel said. "It sure is easier since you got the inside bathroom, Mama."

She followed Faith through the house to the small back room where Faith slept. Once inside she closed the door. "What's going on, sis?" Jewel asked.

"I want to tell you about Davis."

Jewel nodded, encouraging her to continue.

"Mama's been real upset since Davis came. I don't know what he said to her but she was all excited about him coming. She had Paw kill two chickens to cook and she made a coconut cake," Faith said.

"So? Everybody knows fried chicken and coconut cake are Davis's favorites. Why would that upset mama?" Jewel answered, pretending ignorance.

"That's not all. She washed everything in this room. She even washed down the walls, and she's got jars of baby food and that white powder that Judith likes in her coffee hid in the closet."

"So what are you saying? Jewel asked. "What happened? Why did Davis go to Faye's?"

"I'm saying Mama was really looking forward to Davis and Judith being here. I'm saying she spent money buying all kinds of things she would never buy for anyone else. I'm saying Davis and Judith did something bad when they got here," Faith answered.

Jewel was beginning to think she understood her mama's odd behavior. "What do you mean bad?" she asked.

"I don't know. You know Mama don't talk about things to me. All I know is Mama never misses Wednesday night prayer meeting but she did that night. She stayed here and waited on them to get here. She sent us on to church. We all expected them to be here, but when we got home they'd been here and gone. I know they said something bad to her 'cause Mama was crying when we got home."

"Mama crying?" Jewel asked. "Are you sure? Mama don't ever cry."

"Yeah, well. She was crying that night. I guess I know crying when I see it."

"OK, OK. I know you know crying. It's just whatever could he have said to upset her that badly?"

"I think he must have hurt her feelings. I tried to talk to her but she won't talk about it. She just starts making excuses for why he went to Faye's instead of staying here," Faith answered.

Jewel went back to the kitchen where her mama and Gladys sat talking. "So, Mama, how's Judith taking to living back here? She always said she was never leaving California."

Her mama looked down to where her hands were folded on top of the table. "Fine. I guess she likes it fine."

"What does she say? How about the baby? Is she OK? How does Judith handle being around strangers after what happened?"

Gladys looked curiously at her sister. Their mama's eyes began to fill with tears. "I don't know anything about them. They were here only a few minutes, but they didn't want to stay." She paused for a moment, trying to gain control of her voice. "They've not been back."

Gladys spoke up. "Why didn't they stay here, Mama? I know you went to a lot of trouble to get things ready for them."

"Oh, it wasn't no trouble. I just was hoping to have the baby here for a few days, that's all."

"Well, that don't sound right to me," Jewel said. "Davis has no business being so..." She paused trying to find the right word. "So snooty."

"Oh now, girls, Davis is not snooty. He had good reasons, I'm sure. We don't need to be gossiping."

Both girls knew that the conversation was over, at least until they were away from their mama.

By the time Jewel and Gladys arrived back at their homes, they had discussed Davis's alleged insult to their mama in great detail, each one adding her version of what had happened. By the end of the next day, they had given their brother Gerald their account of the story and, during the next week, the story was repeated to all of the family members. Faye's reaction was to tell Jewel she wasn't interested in foolishness.

Each time the story was repeated, it was embellished. The story found its way to the cousins and then on to some of the people living in Piney. Soon enough, it would have been hard for Althea Barnes to recognize this story as being about the evening Davis had arrived from California. Davis, now living twenty miles away and busy getting ready to begin his new job, would not have recognized his character in the story either.

Finally, Althea had seen and heard enough and she decided it was time the whole matter was over and forgotten. She pulled out the box of stationery Loretta had given her last Christmas and began to write.

Dear Children,

Since all of my children seem to have forgotten how brothers and sisters are supposed to treat each other, I guess I have failed somewhere along the way. You are all grown and have busy lives and I don't expect you to come together to hear what I have to say, so I will settle for writing to each of you instead.

I can only tell you how disappointed I am in the way all of you have been behaving these past few weeks, gossiping and carrying tales. I'm ashamed of all of you.

First of all, the most important thing any of you has to do is to teach your children how to behave. Since children learn not from what you say but from the way you act, I ask each of you, what have they learned from you these past weeks?

Each of you should remember that when you sow the seeds of strife and disrespect, your children will learn to be rude and disrespectful.

It is your job to teach your children how to live in peace and avoid strife. Are you doing that? I don't claim to be qualified to tell you how to live. I can only tell you what God's word says. Each of you needs to read your Bible and pray about what has happened.

God has called each of us to be peacemakers. He has told us to make allowances for each other's faults. If any one of you looks hard enough at any other of you, you can find reasons to disagree and you can find something to disapprove of in the other's life. That's called being human beings. Understand that Satan knows what irritates each of us, and he uses that knowledge to cause strife. If you are to be the kind of person you should be, you cannot allow that to happen.

If you are following God's word you will be looking for reasons to approve and love each other instead of criticize and bring down. If, after reading your Bible and praying about this, you decide to rethink your attitudes and actions, I will expect to see you at Faye's house for Thanksgiving.

Come early enough to help out. Don't just show up when it's time to eat.

Love, Mama

The letter was not discussed on Thanksgiving Day, even though all of her children and their families were present. None of Althea's children ever forgot its contents.

Over the years, while his family grew, Davis often pulled out the letter and reread it. It became especially important to him after his mama's death.

THE ROBE
Chapter 6

After Ida and Jim went back to Spartenburg, I couldn't get what she'd said about the ring out of my mind. I soon decided to take out Mama's jewelry box. I rifled through it, looking for the ring. "Davis, do you know where Mama's ring is?" I asked after not finding it in the box.

"What? No, I haven't seen it. Have you looked in your mama's old jewelry box? Isn't that where you keep it?"

"I've looked. It's not there."

"I just don't know, honey. Try to remember where you saw it last."

I rummaged through my mind, searching for when I last saw it. "Ida Mae and I had it out of the box when she was here over the Fourth. I can't remember seeing it after that day. I'm sure it was in the box then."

"Well then, why not call Ida and see what she remembers? Maybe she'll remember something that you can't."

"I guess I could."

Ida answered on the third ring. "Hello."

"Hey, Ida. How's everyone there today?" Before she could answer, I said, "I need your help. Can you remember what we did with Mama's ring when you were here last?"

"I don't know, Judith. I thought you put it back into the jewelry box. Have you looked there?"

"Yeah. I looked in the box but it's not there."

"Well, I don't know. Have you looked in the robe you had on? Could you have put it in one of the pockets?"

"I don't know. I don't remember but I guess it's possible." I hated the spot of suspicion I felt. We talked awhile about other things and I hung up. I began to worry.

"What if I've lost the ring?" I asked Davis.

"You'll find it. Try to stay calm and think. Go through the alphabet and try to remember." Davis thought going through the alphabet looking for something to trigger a memory was always the answer to anything lost.

"Maybe I did put it in the robe." I went into the bedroom to look through Davis' closet. It was his robe, an old one he never wore. Any time it was a little chilly I reached for that robe. After looking for a few moments, I called out to him. "Davis, where's your robe?"

"What robe?"

"You know, the one I like to wear."

"Oh, if you referring to the old pea green thing that makes you look like a fuzzy cabbage head, I gave it away."

"You gave away my robe?"

"It was mine and, yes, I gave it away. I gave it to the Salvation Army when they came to pick up the couch. You can wear the new satin robe I bought you for Christmas."

"Why do you need it?"

"Well, Ida thinks I may have put the ring in one of the pockets."

"I hope not. There's no telling where it is by now."

I made a face at him.

Over the weekend I searched the house over and over again, but the ring was nowhere to be found. On Monday I found myself driving on the street where the Salvation Army building was located. Might as well check it out, I told myself.

I wandered through the store, hoping to see the pea green robe hanging on one of the racks.

"Can I help you?"

I turned to see a small middle-aged woman standing beside me. She was well dressed. I guessed she was a volunteer. "I don't know," I said. "I'm looking for a robe."

"Well, we have several. I'm sure we can find one to fit. You're a medium. Am I right?"

"No, I mean yes, I'm a medium but I'm not looking for a robe to wear." I stopped talking when I saw she looked puzzled. "It's a long story," I said. "My husband sent the robe along when you had our couch picked up last week. I mean he sent several things and one of them was the robe. I need to find it and check the pockets." I was beginning to get flustered. "Look, I think I may have left my mama's ring in one of the pockets. I don't want the robe back but I would love to find the ring."

"Couch, couch, now let me think, couch. Was it a sleeper sofa?"

"Yes, it was beige with tiny brown leaves."

"I remember the couch. I'm the one who checked the goods in. I think I still have the list here somewhere. Let me see." She led the way to the counter and rummaged through the drawer. "Let's see, it's here somewhere. Oh, yes. Here it is: couch, two shirts, a jacket, three pairs of slacks. There's no robe. That's strange. If the robe had come into the building it would have been recorded."

"I don't understand. My husband gave it to the person who picked up the couch."

"I'll tell you what. The driver that day was Jack Lawson, and I believe he's here today. I'll just go in the back and see if he's still in the building." She went through a door into what I thought was probably the storeroom. I waited, wondering if Davis had been mistaken.

After a few moments a small, wiry dark-haired man came through the storeroom door. "Hello, I'm Jack Lawson. I understand you have a question about a pick-up I made?"

"Yes, you picked up a couch and some clothes at my house last week. I need to find one piece of clothing. It was a green robe."

He thought a moment and sighed. "The pea green robe. Yes, I remember it. It was in pretty good shape and looked to be real warm."

"That's it. That's the one. Where is it? I really need to find it."

He walked to the storeroom door and peeked inside then looked around the immediate area. "I didn't bring it here. I gave it to an old lady on the street. Look, I can get in trouble for giving things away without going through the channels but, you see, some of those people out there won't come in here or anyplace else, so I sometimes take things to them, if you know what I mean?"

"Do you know who she is? Can you help me find her?"

"I don't know. I don't know her name, but I guess I can take you to where she usually stays."

"When? I mean can we go now?"

He looked at his watch. "I'll be leaving here in thirty minutes. If you want to wait I'll take you there."

The part of town where Jack led me was certainly not the most affluent. The buildings were smeared with graffiti, and all bars covered all the windows. He stopped at a corner where several street people milled around. "Where can I find Hattie?" he yelled to a group sitting on the stairs of a building.

"Who wants to know?" one of the men answered roughly.

"Hey, Mr. Jack," another called. "Come on over and join us. I'll share a drink with you, if you bring the drink that is."

"No thanks, Harry. I'll take a rain check. Today I'm looking for Hattie. Can you help me?"

"Yeah, well, she's gone to live with her daughter up in Oregon. She'll not be spending any more nights on the street I guess."

"Oregon? How did that happen?" I walked to where the two men sat sharing a bottle wrapped in a brown paper bag.

"I don't know except this woman showed up a couple days ago and seemed all excited to find ole Hattie. She cried a lot until she finally had Hattie loaded into her station wagon and took off," he said.

"Do you know her name? It's kind of important that we find her," Jack said.

"As a matter of fact, maybe I can help you." He dug into his pocket and began pulling out an assortment of string, cans, marbles, bottle lids and other treasures. Finally, he pulled out a small piece of a business card. "Ah, here it is. This fell out of the car." He handed the scrap to Jack.

"Thanks, Harry," Jack said. "I'll be by to see you tomorrow. I'm making a pick-up over in Greenewood." Jack waved to the men and walked back to my car. "Here, miss. I hope this helps."

When he drove away, I looked down at the scrap of a card. The name was torn off, but part of the address and all of the phone number were still visible.

HATTIE [THREE MONTHS EARLIER]
Chapter 7

The Greyhound bus station in downtown Memphis was empty except for the night desk clerk, two soldiers waiting for the next bus to Atlanta, and an old woman asleep on a bench near the doorway. The bus for Atlanta pulled into the terminal, and a dozen passengers got off and filed into the station. Each one collected an odd assortment of baggage and hurried out of the building. The hustle of taxis and family cars picking up the passengers soon disappeared. The two soldiers climbed into the bus and, once again, the station was quiet. The old woman slept through the commotion without stirring.

"Ma'am, ma'am, are you OK?" The desk clerk gently shook the woman's shoulder. "Ma'am, are you waiting on a bus? There's no more due in till tomorrow morning at seven o'clock. It's after two in the morning."

"What? What do you want?" Hattie shrieked, pulling back from the desk clerk.

"I'm sorry to startle you, ma'am, but there's no more buses coming in tonight."

"Bus? What do you mean bus? I don't need a bus. Where am I?" The woman was obviously confused and frightened.

"You're in Memphis. You're in the Memphis, Tennessee, bus terminal, ma'am. You came in on the seven-thirty bus from Arkansas. Are you waiting on someone?" he asked urgently. "Do you need help?"

"No, I don't think so. Who are you? Do I know you?"

"My name is Lawrence Steelwood. I'm the night station manager here. Do you want me to call a taxi for you?"

"Taxi? Taxi? Yes, call me a taxi."

"Wait here." The station manager walked to the desk to make a call. When he returned the woman had not moved from the bench. "I called a taxi. It's driven by a friend of mine. Just tell him where you want to go and he'll take care of you." The station manager slipped onto the bench beside the woman. "Ma'am, are you sure you're OK? Do you have family here in Memphis? Can I call someone for you?"

"Family? I guess I must have," the woman muttered. "Where did you say this is?" "Memphis, you're in Memphis, Tennessee. What's your name, ma'am?"

"Hattie, my name's Hattie."

The door opened, admitting the taxi driver. "This is Hattie," the station manager said. "She needs to go to the Saint Christopher Mission. Hattie, this is a friend of mine. He'll take care of you."

The driver nodded in understanding. "Hello Hattie," he said calmly. "If you're ready I'll take you to where you can get a good night's sleep, and then tomorrow I'll help you find your family. Now, how does that sound?".

Hattie allowed herself to be helped into the taxi. She

sat silently while the taxi traveled the five blocks to the Saint Christopher Mission. She stared out the window, ignoring the taxi driver's attempts at conversation. Once they arrived, he opened her door and led Hattie up the steps and into the mission.

Once inside the mission, the taxi driver led Hattie to one of the chairs lined up along the wall. He looked up as another woman entered the room. She was dressed in the gray habit of a nun-in-training. "Good evening, Phillip." She sat down in the chair beside Hattie, who was frowning and wringing her hands. She offered her hand to Hattie. "Hello, I'm Sister Lucinda." Hattie tentatively took the nun's hand. Lucinda clasped both hands around Hattie's.

Once Hattie had eaten and was settled into a small room for the night, Lucinda sat behind her desk examining the contents of Hattie's purse. She copied the information from Hattie's billfold onto a yellow pad. She replaced the card and peeked into the bill compartment. My goodness, Hattie, she said to herself. "You're not our typical homeless person, are you? Two hundred and fifty dollars." She replaced the money and closed the purse. "I'll call the police in the morning. Someone has surely reported Hattie as missing."

Hattie awoke around five in the morning. The room was not familiar. Where was she anyway? She recovered her coat from the chair where it lay and pulled it on. Her shoes and purse were nearby. She slipped into her shoes and clutched her purse tightly to her chest. The stairs creaked as she hurried down the street. Where was she? What was this place?

It was Hattie Williams's first day on the street. Her

first day as a homeless person.

She bought a bagel with cream cheese in a small café then headed back onto the street. For the next ten hours Hattie alternated between walking aimlessly and sitting confused, scared, and alone on the curb or, whenever possible, on a park bench.

When nightfall came she found shelter behind a thick grouping of bushes in the city park. Before daylight came again her purse was gone. The thief had slipped up to where Hattie slept, grabbed the purse, and run away.

When Hattie awoke she barely noticed the purse was missing. As she gathered her coat tightly around her, against the morning chill, the purse was quickly forgotten. Hattie was luckier than most people thrust into surviving on the street. She was alive and, for the next six weeks, she would somehow survive. When her daughter Marion finally found her, she was dirty and confused but otherwise OK.

The nine acres surrounding the Harkenship Clinic would rival any five-star resort and spa. The grounds were divided into three types of landscaping, each different but blending together perfectly. The four acres furthest from the building were heavily wooded. The large hardwood trees—oak, beech, and maple—shared the landscape with cedars and white pines.

A stone pathway snaked in and out of the tall trees. Along the pathway several benches gave guests a place to rest and watch an assortment of small animals play. Near the edge of the wooded area, a rock wall provided the source of a stream that dominated the next three acres. As if by magic, water gushed out from the top of the fifteen-foot rock wall into a manmade stream bed.

Both large and small rocks spaced along the streambed gave the moving water the appearance of a rushing mountain stream.

Once past these rocks the water poured over a smaller waterfall and into a round pond. The pond measured some eighteen feet across and was stocked with an assortment of brightly colored fish. Once the water passed through the pond, it ran underground and across the manicured third section of the grounds until it reached a large round fountain that sat squarely in the center of three acres of flower beds, rose trellises, and groomed shrubbery. Tucked in secluded shady hideaways, among the sweet-smelling beds of flowers, were more benches where guests could relax.

One of these garden benches was Hattie's favorite place to spend the afternoon. Since she'd come back to Harkenship, she remembered very little of the time she'd spent outside. Outside was scary. Outside was cold. The people here were not unkind to her, so she didn't know why she'd left in the first place. She held up her hand up and looked at the ring she wore. The black stone glittered when the sun touched it. "My that's a pretty ring, Hattie," a nurse said, sitting down on the bench beside her.

"Yes, ain't it though?" Hattie smiled and turned the ring to catch the light.

"Where did you get it? Did your daughter Marion give it to you?"

"Yes, well no, I'm not sure. I suppose she must have but I don't know. I think I might have found it."

"Well, I don't suppose it matters much." The nurse patted Hattie's hand. "It's yours now and it looks beautiful on your hand."

Hattie smiled happily, looking at the ring.

"Do you want a book to read? I brought several for you to choose from."

"No, I think I'll just sit and enjoy the day."

The nurse stood up to leave. "I'm glad you came back, Hattie. We missed you."

Left alone Hattie watched the birds in the trees near the bench for a while until her attention was caught by a young woman sitting beside a small fish pond. She was looking into the water, occasionally stirring it lightly with her fingertips. Hattie wondered about her. She knew the girl had been brought here after a failed suicide attempt. Hattie wondered what could possibly cause a beautiful young girl like that to attempt to take her own life.

KATHY

Chapter 8

Kathy made circles in the water with her hand and then watched as they became larger and larger until they disappeared into the pond's edge. That's my life, she thought. At first it's big and meaningful, but then it gets to be less and less till it disappears. She stared across the garden and saw Hattie sitting alone on the bench. "Look at her. Dropped off here and left alone to die." She stood up and walked toward the main hospital building, passing close to where Hattie sat.

"Sometimes the best thing a person can do for themself is to find a quiet place to be alone. Sometimes people need friends to talk to," Hattie said to her.

Kathy stopped and looked at Hattie; then she just walked away. I don't need your problems too, she thought.

Kathy was the only child left to Katherine and Barry Rosen. Her younger brother, Cal, had died five weeks earlier when a fire destroyed her parents' home in Burlington, Oregon. Cal had been a Down's syndrome child, and caring for him had taken up all of her time. She'd had no time for herself. Perhaps the fire had been intentional. She'd wished him gone so many times. No, she didn't intend for him to die. It was not her fault. She didn't mean for anything to happen. It was an accident. Surely they couldn't blame her, or could they? She just didn't know. Her mother had screamed at her and accused her of wanting Cal dead. Kathy had found her room inside the Harkenship Clinic and closed herself inside. The wounds from her suicide attempt were still fresh and raw.

Her wrist hurt badly but not nearly as much as the hurt she felt inside. Her mother had screamed at her and accused her of killing her brother. Poor Cal. Poor sweet, dumb Cal.

Kathy had been twelve when her mother had become pregnant with Cal. Her mom had not been happy to be having another child at that particular time in her life. Kathy had been in the first grade when her mom had gone back to finish her college degree. She'd quit when she'd become pregnant with Kathy and stayed at home with her. By the time Kathy was in the fourth grade, her mom had earned a master's degree in psychology. She took a job with a social service clinic and continued her education. When Kathy was nine her mom borrowed $100,000 and opened her own clinic. A year later she was pregnant.

"I can't be," she shrieked at her husband. Kathy could hear the noise from her room. I've just borrowed a lot of money. It's not fair. I don't want another child."

After all of the weeping and wailing had ended, she was still pregnant. She continued working right up until time for the baby to be born. Kathy was anxious to see the baby. She didn't know if it would be a boy or a girl before the birth. Her mom refused to be checked. Kathy's dad tried to encourage her mom to furnish a nursery, but after several loud, nasty scenes, he'd given up and quit mentioning the child.

Cal was born in December, just five days after Kathy turned eleven and three days before Christmas. Her mom and dad brought him home on Christmas Day. Afterwards her mother never held him except when she had no choice. She hired a sitter and returned to work within a week of his birth.

For a while Kathy's dad tried to adjust, both to the less than perfect baby and his increasingly angry wife. He soon began staying away from home more and more and, by the time Cal celebrated his second birthday, he'd left for good. Kathy felt the loss of her father keenly. She'd felt close to him, and he'd called her his princess. He'd stopped calling her that soon after Cal's birth.

Kathy didn't blame her dad for leaving. Since Cal's birth her mom had screamed at him and she'd screamed at Kathy and she'd screamed at God. "Why did you do this to me?"

Kathy went into Cal's room every night to rock him to sleep. She sang to him and played "one little piggy, two little piggy." After her dad left there was only Kathy and the sitter to care for Cal. Her mom never came home before eight o'clock. By that time Kathy had usually put Cal to bed. The sitter always left at six so, day after day, Kathy was left alone with the baby till her mother arrived at eight or nine. She missed her dad.

By the time Cal was four years old, Kathy had almost lost all contact with her father. He remarried and his visits become less and less frequent. When he asked Kathy to come to his new home in Saint Lewis, she refused. She tried to explain to him about Cal, but he dismissed her reasoning as a childish attempt to hurt him. Cal was not important to him, and he didn't understand her devotion to her less than perfect brother.

Kathy was now sixteen and in high school. Even though she loved Cal, she began to want to spend time with friends her own age. She had no social life after six at night, when Cal's sitter left for home. There was no one else to take care of him. One day Johnny Bailey asked her to go to the movies, and she desperately wanted to accept. Johnny Bailey was just about the coolest boy ever. She asked her mom to be home by six thirty so she could go. Her mother had promised to be there on time.

Johnny arrived at seven but her mom was still not home. At seven thirty Kathy put Cal in his crib and told him not to get up. Cal was afraid to get out of his crib by himself, so Kathy knew he'd be OK; besides, her mom would be home any time.

That night, when Cal called out for Kiki, she didn't answer. That night, when Cal decided to climb out of his crib and find Kiki, he found the box of matches that Kathy had left in her room. A box of matches she used to light the candles that Cal loved to watch burn.

Kathy couldn't enjoy the movie. At eight thirty she called home. Her mom didn't answer the phone. As the minutes passed she began to feel more and more concerned until, at nine o'clock, she abruptly jumped out of her seat and announced to an astonished Johnny that she had to go home. When they turned the corner at her block, she saw the fire truck and the ambulance.

That was five weeks ago. Since coming to the clinic, she'd spent most days out in the garden beside the small fish pond. She'd seen the old woman sitting on the same bench every day. Today was no different. Kathy made her way to the fish pond as soon as her morning session with the doctor was over. She sat watching the fish and contemplating the things the doctor had said to her that morning.

"They say fish live strictly by instinctive behavior, but I'm not so sure about it," Hattie said. She was standing behind Kathy, who sat looking into the water. Hattie knelt down, put her hand in the water, and flicked her finger three times. The fish converged on her hand, and she released the flakes of fish food. "Do you think they come to my hand by instinct? I don't."

Hattie walked back across the lawn to the bench, where she sat down and turned her attention to the birds. Kathy wondered about the old woman. Often, during the next few days, her thoughts strayed to her. Kathy became more and more curious.

One day she left her session with the doctor and headed toward the pond, but when she saw the old woman, she stopped. Kathy stood beside the bench without speaking. After a few moments, she sat down on the bench. "What did you do to be put in here? Did you kill someone too?" Kathy asked defiantly.

"No, I don't think so. I don't remember it if I did. I'm here because I forget to take my medicine and when I don't take it, I forget who or what I am. I have a daughter and a home but I forgot all about it. This time she found me in Memphis, Tennessee, living on the street. They tell me I was missing for six weeks. I don't remember. When I'm here they make sure I take my medicine." Hattie didn't look at the girl.

"So you're just crazy," Kathy snapped.

Hattie shrugged. They sat in silence for a few

moments longer.

Kathy finally broke the silence. "Were you born crazy? I mean some people are born with things wrong with them."

"I don't know," Hattie answered. "I guess it's possible. I was married and raised a daughter. I think I was normal all those years." There were a few more moments of silence. "I became sick after Kenneth died," Hattie said. "My husband Kenneth, that is."

"I'll bet your daughter's ashamed of you. I'll bet she wishes you were dead," Kathy said.

"I'm sure she is sometimes ashamed of me, and I imagine there are times when she gets really tired and upset with me and thinks she'd be happier if I just disappeared. Those are just human feelings. They don't make her a bad daughter, nor do they make her responsible for my illness. I know that she loves me even though my illness has caused her many heartaches."

"So you say," Kathy muttered and walked toward the pond.

Hattie didn't see Kathy for the next couple of days. Then one morning she was sitting on the garden bench again, feeding the birds, when Kathy stormed out through the clinic door and across the lawn. She walked directly to Hattie. "I want to forget I ever had a family. I want to walk out of here with every moment of my life erased. Tell me how I can do that?"

Hattie turned to look at Kathy's face. "Come and sit down. It's hard for an old woman to twist around to see you." She patted the seat beside her.

"What's it like to not be able to remember anything

about who you are or where you came from?" Kathy asked.

"Well, I don't exactly know. I can't remember anything about it except fear. A constant overpowering fear." Hattie reached over and patted Kathy's hand. "Do you want to tell me about how you come to be here, child?"

Kathy shook her head. Tears began to form in her eyes. They spilled over and streaked down her cheeks. She began to talk. "I killed my brother. I didn't mean to but it was my fault. Sometimes I wanted him to disappear but not usually. Usually I loved him. I was the only family he had."

Once Kathy began talking she didn't stop until she'd told Hattie the whole story about Cal and his tragic death.

"You know, Kathy. You didn't do anything bad. You made a bad decision but we all do that once in a while. I believe your brother loved you and you made his four years of life happy ones. I think maybe you were more of a mother to him than a sister. It wasn't your fault he was born not perfect. It wasn't your mother or father's fault either. Those things happen sometimes. The important thing is you loved him and he knew it. You're not the bad guy in all of this," Hattie said softly. "Both you and your brother were victims, but you don't have to keep on being one. You can't change anything about Cal's death by wishing it had not happened. You can't change your parents' divorce by wishing things were back the way they were before, but you can control your future. It's all up to you, child."

Kathy listened. She listened more closely than she had listened to anything her doctor had said. She listened and believed. Over the next two weeks, Kathy spent her days with Hattie. Most days they didn't talk about their past. Some days they barely spoke; they just sat or walked together on the clinic grounds, one or both of them reading. "The doctor says I can go home tomorrow," Kathy said one morning. "They say I'm ready to leave here."

"Why Kathy, that's wonderful!"

"I don't know if I'm ready. I don't know if I want to," Kathy stammered.

"My goodness, child, don't say that. You're ready to leave and you've got so much to experience. It's time you got on with your life, child."

"I'm not sure, Hattie. I don't know how I feel about living with Mom. I still have a lot of bad feelings toward her, but I sure don't want to live with Dad and his new wife either."

"You know, Kathy, there are three things you have to do before you can leave things behind and go on. One, you have to forgive yourself. Next, you have to forgive your mother and father; then you have to forgive God. Not that God needs anyone's forgiveness, mind you, but then forgiving is not for the forgiven. It is for the forgiver." Hattie spoke to Kathy in much the same way she had spoken to her own daughter, years earlier, when she was a teenager. "Now I've got something I want to give you. Do you remember I told you about finding a ring when I was living on the street? In no time after finding it, my daughter came to get me. I call it my good luck ring and I want you to have it." She held the ring up in the sunlight, allowing the sun's rays to make the stone sparkle. This ring made my daughter find me. This is a lucky ring," she said firmly.

Kathy looked down at the ring then toward Hattie's face. She could tell the old woman truly believed the ring had power.

"Who told you the ring was lucky?" Kathy asked.

"No one told me, child. I just know it. This is a lucky ring."

"I don't know, Hattie. That ring is important to you."

"I'd really like for you to have it," Hattie insisted. "Besides it'll make you remember me."

"Thanks, Hattie, but I don't need a ring to remember you," Kathy said.

Hattie removed the ring from her finger and closed it into Kathy's fist. "Write and let me know how you're doing, OK? I know everything will be OK with you. God will make a way for you and, besides, you have my lucky ring now." Hattie patted Kathy's hand affectionately.

THE SEARCH
Chapter 9

I carried the torn business card into the kitchen and stuck it to the side of the refrigerator with an apple magnet. Then I searched through Mama's jewelry box again and again. "Well it won't cost me anything but a phone call," I muttered, pulling the card off the refrigerator.

"Hello."

"Hello. My name is Judith Barnes. I hope you can help me. You see, I'm looking for my mother's ring.

"I'm sorry but you must have the wrong number."

"Wait, I'm sorry. I guess I started off wrong. I live in Memphis, Tennessee, and I was given your business card by a gentleman who found it when it fell out of your car. You came to Memphis to pick up your mother." There was nothing but silence on the other end of the phone, so I began talking again.

"I know this might sound a little strange, but I believe your mother was given a robe by a gentleman from the Salvation Army. I'm hoping to find her. I think my mother's ring may have been in one of the pockets of that robe."

Finally, after what seemed like forever, she spoke.

"This is a surprise. I, uh, I did go to Memphis to get my mother a few weeks ago, but I don't know anything about a ring. I'm in the middle of something right now, but if you'll give me your number I'll call you back at a later time."

"Oh yes. That would be great. Thank you," I said hurriedly. After giving her the number, I hung up the phone and went outside to where Davis was working. "Well, I'll probably never hear from her."

"What are you mumbling about? Who won't you hear from?" Davis asked.

"Oh, I called the number on the card about Mama's ring, but the lady who answered was not exactly helpful."

"Why, what did she say?"

"Oh, she said she'd call me back when she had time."

"That doesn't sound so bad. Don't give up."

Two days later she called. "Ms. Barnes, this is Marion Webb. I'm sorry to have taken so long to get back with you, but I may be able to give you some information about the ring you're looking for."

"Great, oh that would be wonderful. Do you have my ring?"

"No, as a matter of fact I don't, but I may be able to help you. My mother was wearing a ring when I picked her up. Can you describe it?"

"It is gold with a black stone. That's the ring your mother has, isn't it?"

"Yes, that's the ring."

"That's great. If you could mail it to me, I'd be

grateful."

"Wait, wait a minute. I don't have the ring. My mother does. She calls it her lucky ring. I'll pay you whatever it's worth. She's so attached to the ring. I don't want to ask her to give it up."

"No, no I can't do that. Listen, that ring was passed down to my mother from her mother and from her mother before that. No, I don't want to sell my mother's ring."

"Well, I guess I can understand that. I'll go see Mom and get the ring. I'll call you when I do. Goodbye, Ms. Barnes."

As soon as I hung up the phone, I hurried to tell Davis and call Ida Mae.

The next day Marion Webb phoned to say her mother no longer had the ring. "I'm sorry, Ms. Barnes, but she gave it to a young girl she befriended at the clinic."

"What do you mean she gave the ring away?" I yelled. "You said she had it."

"Yes, I know I told you that but she doesn't have it anymore. She gave it away. I'm sorry."

"Who did she give it to?" I demanded, feeling the anger rise inside me. Incompetence, God how I hate incompetence.

"Oh, some girl from the clinic where she was being treated. Mom thinks the ring brings good luck, and she said the girl needed some. The girl's brother had just died in a fire. Look, I'm sorry but the ring is gone. Mother's not well and she's convinced the ring has some kind of power to help protect the girl."

I didn't know what to say to that. "OK, I understand."

"Listen, Ms. Barnes, I'll see what I can find out about the girl, OK? Maybe she'll be willing to give it back."

Later I told Davis about the phone call and the latest in the ring's saga.

"That's amazing, Judith. It almost sounds as if the ring has a mind of its own." Davis laughed. I laughed along with him, but afterwards I began to wonder about it myself.

Ida Mae will love this, I thought as I dialed her number.

"Wow, maybe Davis is right," Ida said excitedly after I repeated the story to her. "I sure would love to know more about where the ring came from. Maybe it does have some sort of power." We talked awhile longer and then hung up after I promised to keep her updated.

Over the next few days, I became more and more intrigued by the possibilities I imagined for the ring. Ida and Bill were scheduled to come for Thanksgiving, so I put my fascination with Mama's ring on hold while I cleaned the house and prepared for the coming holiday.

After supper on Thanksgiving Day, Ida and I talked while we cleaned the kitchen. "I called Uncle Floyd last week," she said.

"You did? How are he and Aunt Agnes?"

Uncle Floyd was our dad's only brother, but we had never been close to him. He and Aunt Agnes married and moved to Iowa before I was born. Ida Mae was probably closer to him than any of our brothers and sisters because she was the oldest and could remember him before his marriage to Aunt Agnes.

"They were both OK. Do you remember his son Andy? He and Ruth live there on the farm now. Uncle Floyd said he and Agnes just piddle around the garden and spoil the grandchildren now. Andy and Ruth work the farm.

"I remember Andy and Ruth from Mama's funeral, but I don't think I saw their kids."

"They didn't bring them to the funeral," Ida said. "Anyway, the reason I called was to see if Uncle Floyd could remember anything about Mama's mother, Granny Helton."

"Whatever for?"

"The ring, Judith. Granny Helton was Andrea Baker's daughter. Don't you see? I'm trying to see if there may be something written down somewhere about the ring being special."

"Special? By special are you meaning special like in magic? Come on, Ida," I said teasingly.

"Don't laugh, Judith. Even you will have to admit there's something strange about the ring."

"I'll tell you what, Ida. Let's both take a look at the papers Mom left in her desk and maybe her Bible. I've got her papers stored in a box in the top of the hall closet. I'll get that." I pretended to humor Ida but, secretly, I was interested. I had cleaned out Mama's desk after her death without looking through any of the papers.

Ida Mae and I sat down in the middle of the living room floor and began searching through the papers. After a couple of hours we'd found mortgage papers for the house we grew up in, several loan contracts for cars, letters from Uncle Paul, and love letters Dad wrote while he was stationed in the Navy, but nothing about the ring.

"Well. It was a good idea." Ida's disappointment was obvious.

"What, giving up already?" I teased. "We still have her Bible and there's all those boxes up in the attic." I left Ida sitting on the floor, in the midst of all the papers and photos we'd pulled out of the box, and went to retrieve Mama's Bible from her dresser.

"Why do you keep it there?" Ida asked when she saw me pull it from the dresser drawer.

"Oh, I don't know. I guess I worry it'll get damaged if I leave it out." I sat down beside her, in the midst of the papers, and opened the book. Mama's Bible was old and big, much bigger than any other I'd seen. It was bound in white leather that had yellowed with age. In her neat script, Mama had recorded her brothers' and sisters' births as well as Uncle Paul's and Dad's deaths. I turned the pages, reading the handwritten record of Mama's family. Each part was written by a different hand. Both of us were fascinated by the history recorded there.

"I wonder why we never took the time to read this before?" Ida asked.

"I don't know. Mama always kept it put up out of sight."

"Look here," Ida said suddenly. "Here's Andrea Baker's name, and look here. Here's the record of her death, August 12, 1890. What's this, Judith?" She scraped her fingernail across an ink-smeared line. "It looks like something's been marked out." We held the Bible up to the light, turning it this way and that, trying to make out the writing.

"What in the world are you two doing?" It was Davis speaking. He and Bill had come into the room.

"Somebody has written something here and then marked it out," I answered. "We're trying to read it."

Davis peered over our shoulders at the page we were trying to read. "Maybe I can help." He left the room and came back, a few minutes later, carrying a sheet of onion-skin paper and a crayon. He laid the paper over the page and began carefully rubbing across it. As if by magic words began to appear. "May God have mercy on her soul for I have none to spare nor room in my heart to forgive."

"Who could have written that?" I asked.

"My guess would be it was written by your great-grandfather, Andrea Baker's husband. I'd also guess the Bible came down from his family," Davis said smugly.

Ida Mae and I looked at each other. "I wonder if there's anything else in here?" she said excitedly.

We both began searching through the pages in earnest, but we found nothing more.

"Well that's that," I said. We both slumped against the back of the couch. After a few moments I remembered Uncle Floyd. "When you talked to Uncle Floyd, did he know anything?"

"The only thing he could remember was that his mother had a small box she kept in a locked drawer of her nightstand. He saw her open it only once."

"Well, come on, tell me. What was in the box?"

"Nothing really. A small bag with a book of some

kind inside." She shrugged.

"I wonder? Could those have belonged to Andrea Baker?"

"Judith, do you think it could have?" Ida asked. "Do you think Mama had them? If so, they're somewhere in her things."

We both jumped up from the floor and headed toward the stairs that led to the attic. We were running and shoving each other, both trying to be the first to reach the stairs.

Three hours later we had opened and searched through every box. We'd found pictures drawn when we were children, grade cards for all of our brothers and sisters for every year of school, birthday cards, many hand drawn in childish script and a few purchased, and clothes bought for different occasions that had never been worn. We found a lot of things about Mama's life, but no small bag or book.

We went to bed that night disappointed. The next morning when I came downstairs Ida was already there looking through Mama's jewelry box, which was sitting on the kitchen counter. "Judith, I just don't understand this. This is the one thing Mama seemed to prize. If I were her I'd have put it in here. I've looked again and again, but there's just nothing."

We finished breakfast just as my daughter Katrina and granddaughter Angel arrived. "Grandma, Papaw, I'm here." Angel ran to hug my neck. Angel loved me but her papaw was clearly her favorite person in the world, hands down. She soon left me with her mama and aunt Ida and hurried to find her papaw. I could hear them talking and laughing and knew she would quickly find her way into his lap.

After a few minutes Ida and I took Katrina into the living room to show her what we had found in Mama's Bible. Katrina was fascinated by the way her dad had unraveled the mystery of the writing that had been marked through by Joshua Baker. As we passed the doorway leading into the den, we stopped for a moment to watch Angel and Davis. "Do you remember that story?" I asked Katrina when Angel began begging Davis to tell her the story about the shoes.

Katrina smiled. "It was one of my favorites, if I recall." We listened for a moment before continuing into the living room.

"Papaw, you're so warm and soft." Angel snuggled deeper into Davis's lap.

"Soft? What do you mean soft? I'll show you soft. Oh, oh, here comes the claw." Davis teased Angel by raising his hand and slowing forming his fingers into the shape he always did just before he began to tickle her.

Angel squealed and snuggled deeper into the area under her papaw's arm. "Tell me about your shoes again, Papaw," she begged.

"Shoes, shoes? Them weren't shoes, little girl, them were galoshes, red flying galoshes."

"Tell me about them red flying galoshes, Papaw." Angel said, mocking his pronunciation.

FLYING RED GALOSHES
Chapter 10

Davis sat back in his chair and began the story. "Well, you see when I was a little boy my mom and dad didn't have the money to buy shoes for me and all my brothers and sisters to wear. There were thirteen of us altogether and that amounts to a lot of shoes. In the summertime we all went barefoot, but every fall the Presbyterian Church would bring a big box of shoes to the church and we would all go into town to pick out a new pair for the winter. Most of the families in Piney were like us and couldn't afford to buy shoes, so the line to get them from the church was always long."

Angel smiled and nodded encouragement as if she'd never heard the story before.

"If I remember correctly, I was nine years old. It was early October so the weather was beginning to be a mite chilly on our bare feet. This particular year Mama was tied up delivering my brother Stephen, and she left my older sister Faye in charge of all us kids. Well, as it happened, the day came when the church had the box of shoes ready to give out, but my sister Faye just forgot to send us down to the church. It was late afternoon when she finally remembered, so she quickly hurried us off.

"'Davis,' she said, 'you're the oldest. You're responsible for the little ones. Make sure all of them get shoes.'"

We walked the five miles into town; all ten of us were barefoot. When we reached the church building, everyone had already left except one lady.

"'Oh my,' she said when I explained why we had come. 'My goodness, look at you all. Are all of you brothers and sisters?'

"'Yes, ma'am,' I answered. 'I'm the oldest and I'll wait till the last if you don't mind,' I added, hoping to show I was responsible for my brothers and sisters and I took that responsibility seriously.

"'Well,' she said, looking into the box of shoes. 'I don't think we'll have any problem with the younger ones but I have only a couple pair of shoes big enough for you two big boys. I hope they will fit.'

"After a while all of my brothers and sisters were wearing the new shoes she had fitted on them, and it was my turn. She looked into the box and then down at my feet, frowning.

"'Mama says I take after my Uncle Willard. He had big feet too,' I said, trying to explain why my nine-year-old body had such big feet hanging off the end of my skinny legs.

"'I don't know, son, none of these shoes will go on your feet,' she said sympathetically.

"I looked into the box. 'Here, I can wear these,' I said, reaching into the box and pulling out a pair of red galoshes. 'These'll fit me. I can tell.'

"'I don't know, son,' she said. 'Those are not shoes for everyday wearing. Those are to wear over your shoes when it rains.'

"I sat down on the floor and pulled the red galoshes on over my bare feet. 'There,' I said. 'They fit me just fine.' As soon as I pulled them onto my feet, I felt something happen, something special that I just couldn't explain. I knew them red galoshes were meant for me. I stood and began walking around the room, raising myself up on my toes and testing the feel of them.

"'I don't think you should be wearing them,' she said. 'I mean not without proper shoes inside them.'

"'These are fine. These will do the trick,' I said, hurrying to get away before she took them back.

"'Well, I guess you can keep them. I'll see what I can do to get you a proper pair next month. I guess they'll have to do till then,' she answered reluctantly.

"We all thanked her and left the church to walk the five miles back home. I felt like I was walking on air in my new red galoshes.

"From that day on I wore them everywhere I went. Don't you tell anyone but sometimes I even slept in them. School was scheduled to start in a week. On the first day I pulled on my new red shoes and tucked my pant legs down inside them so everyone could get the full effect when I walked into the room.

"When Monday came I made my entrance into the seventh grade classroom and, as I did, everyone turned to look. My gang of friends came running over to greet me. Virgil and Kenneth McCormick being the loudest of the group. Across the room Junior Hall stood with his followers standing behind him. He looked me up and down and his eyes settled on my feet.

"He began to laugh. When he did that, his friends

laughed too.

"'What are you looking at?' I asked defiantly. You see Junior was the son of the owner of the only store in town, and he always wore the best clothes and shoes. I could tell by looking that his shiny brown brogans didn't come out of no church box. He took great store in teasing me and my friends because of our patched overalls and give-away shoes.

"'Where'd you get them red galoshes?' he asked, snickering to his friends.

"'I got 'um at the getting place. What's it to you?' I answered, giving him back just as good as I got.

"'Don't you know them ain't real shoes?' he asked.

"'Sure I know these ain't shoes. These are flying red galoshes and I can beat any one of you any time in 'em,' I answered defiantly.

"Junior Hall began to laugh out loud. Of course his clones standing behind him laughed also. One of my friends, Virgil McCormick, spoke up. 'Davis can beat any of youins, runnin' or fightin', and me and Kenneth here'll back him up.

"'None of you have ever beat me at anything,' Junior answered. 'I can outrun you or outfight you anytime, twerk, so don't go running your mouth to me.'

"'Put up or shut up,' I said.

"'Davis Barnes, you know you can't outrun me. You never have and you never will, specially not in those stupid red things,' he challenged, walking over to stand in front of me and shaking his fist just a few inches from my face.

"About that time the teacher came into the room, breaking up the confrontation. 'I'll meet you at recess,' I said, walking away to find my seat.

"Well, the morning passed and it was getting close to recess time. I don't mind telling you I was getting a little scared. You see, Junior was right. He'd always been the fastest boy in the whole class, the best at softball, and he'd always got the best of me anytime our games had ended in a scuffle. I reached down and rubbed the top of my red galoshes to keep my courage up.

"Finally the bell for recess rang, and I hurried out the door and onto the playground, Virgil and Kenneth McCormick close behind me. 'I ain't sure you ought to be doing this,' Virgil said while we waited on Junior and his friends to arrive. 'You've raced him a bunch of times and you ain't never won.'

"'I know. I know,' I answered, 'but I ain't never been wearing these flying red galoshes before.' By this time I was getting real cocky about the whole thing. 'I'm glad you didn't chicken out,' I yelled to Junior when I saw him coming down the schoolhouse steps. 'How'd you like to make a little bet?' I sucked in my breath to calm my heart, pushed out my chest, and walked to where Junior and his friends stood waiting.

"Junior looked me up and down then started to laugh again. Of course his friends joined in. 'I'll tell you what,' he answered. 'I'm so sure I can beat you that I'll bet my shoes against yours.'

"I looked down at his feet. I knew the brown brogans were new. Junior got new shoes three or four times a year. He also had a different pair that he wore to church on Sunday. They were low-cut black ones just like the ones his daddy wore. When I didn't answer quickly, he knew I was having second thoughts. 'What's the matter? Are you a scaredy cat? Scaredy cat, scaredy cat, I'll bet your mama eats rats. You're afraid to bet your red shoes, ain't you?' he goaded. 'I don't really want them for me. I want to win them for my sister. She's always wanted some red ones,' he said, goading me on.

"'It's a bet,' I said, then I spit on my hand and reached out for Junior to do the same. That was the only way to seal a dare and mean it. Once you shook with spit hands there was no backing out.

"Junior's friends began patting his back, already congratulating him on his victory.

"'OK, line up here," Virgil yelled over the noise. 'It'll be the same rules as always. Once across the yard to the creek, then back to here, then once around the school. Whoever crosses this line first is the winner. No crying or welching allowed.'

"We both nodded in agreement as we lined up on the mark Virgil had made in the cinders with the toe of his shoes. I breathed deep to calm my racing heart. When I looked toward Virgil he gave me a thumbs up.

"'Ready, set, go,' Virgil yelled and we were off. We were both running as fast as we possibly could across the field toward the creek. Junior was out in front. I could feel my heels slipping up and down inside the galoshes. I could hear the thump, thump as my heels smacked into the bottom of my shoes with every step.

"By the time we reached the creek, Junior was about five feet in front of me. He turned when he reached the edge and started back toward me. Before I could reach the creek, he passed me going back in the other direction.

I could see his face. He was grinning like he'd already won my red galoshes.

"I kept running, pushing as hard and fast as I could, but by the time we reached the schoolhouse he was about ten feet ahead of me. Junior passed the starting point and his gang of friends wildly cheered him on. I was running as fast as I could. I felt like I was flying but still Junior was faster and pulling further ahead. As Junior started to turn the first corner of the schoolhouse, I saw his feet slide in the cinders. He struggled to keep his balance.

"When I reached the corner my red galoshes gripped the loose cinders and held tight. By the time he reached the second corner of the building, I could see he was not quite as far ahead as before. He reached for the corner of the building as his new brown brogans slid sideways, almost making him fall. Once again I rounded the corner without a slip or slide, my red galoshes holding tight to the loose cinders. I could feel the cinders flying up behind me and hitting the backs of my legs.

"Junior was just reaching the third corner when I caught up with him. He slowed to keep from falling, but I ran full speed without a worry. I knew my red galoshes would hold in the cinders and not let me fall. By the time I reached the fourth and last corner of the schoolhouse, I was in the lead. Junior tried to catch me as we raced by the side of the school, but even in the straightaway his shoes were slipping in the cinders that surrounded the building.

"As I came around the last corner, the rest of the class could see I was in the lead. My friends were jumping up and down, yelling, loudly encouraging me on. I crossed the finish line a good four feet in front of Junior. His friends stood silently in disbelief while Virgil and Kenneth jumped and yelled their congratulations.

"Junior crossed the finish line then turned to look toward where I stood in between Virgil and Kenneth. We could see his friends were whispering to him. 'Uh oh,' Virgil said. 'I guess we'll have to fight 'em to get your shoes.'

"Junior walked slowly over to where we stood. I was still panting from the race. 'I beat you fair and square,' I said before he had a chance to speak. I was trying to read his expression. It looked like I might be going to get whipped. Suddenly his face broke out in a wide grin.

"'I reckon you did.' He reached out and grabbed me by the shoulder then slid his arm up to catch my head. He pulled my head close to his chest, and I could feel the punch I knew he was going to throw. Instead he dropped his arm across my shoulder in something akin to a hug. 'I reckon you beat me red. I do believe you're right about them shoes you're wearing. They sure are flying red galoshes,' he said, speaking like he and I were best friends. 'Now come on, let's play a game of ball. How about you being on my team. It's time we showed them eighth grade boys how the game is played.'"

Angel cheered when the story ended. "And you and Junior were friends ever after," she declared.

"Yes, honey, Junior and I were friends ever after. Now go on in the kitchen and eat your breakfast before Grandma gets cranky and comes in here after me."

Angel jumped down from Davis's lap but stopped before going into the kitchen. "Papaw," she asked. "What about the shoes?"

"The shoes? Do you mean Junior's brown shoes or my red galoshes?" Papaw asked.

"Junior's shoes, Papaw. Did you take Junior's shoes?"

Papaw smiled at Angel. "No, sweetheart, I didn't take his shoes. I told him I didn't need his shoes since I had my red galoshes."

Angel appeared to think about that for a minute. "I'm glad you didn't take his shoes, Papaw," she said before running out of the den and into the kitchen, where I had her cereal waiting.

"Grandma, can you come and help me?" Angel called from the kitchen. Katrina and I had left her there at the counter eating a bowl of Rice Krispies. Angel loved the sounds the cereal made when her I poured the milk over it. "Snap, crackle pop," the TV commercial said.

"I'm coming," I yelled and left to see what she needed. When I entered the kitchen, she was standing beside the counter. Tears filled her blue eyes. "I'm sorry, Grandma. I broke your box."

"What box, honey? It's OK. Tell me what happened. Show Grandma the broken box."

She pulled the jewelry box from behind her back. In one hand she held a panel that had come from the bottom of the jewelry box. She held both out to me, tears rolling down her cheeks. I pulled her into my arms along with the box. "Don't cry, baby. It's nothing important." I turned the jewelry box over to see where the panel would fit and there, taped to the inside of the opening, was a small black velvet bag. I gently pulled the bag loose from the tape.

"What is it, Grandma?" Angel asked.

"I think you may have solved our mystery, honey. Go get your mom and Aunt Ida, please." I opened the bag and pulled out a small leather-bound book. Inside the front cover was a piece of paper folded to fit and yellowed with age.

I opened the note and began reading. "Dear Joshua, Please don't discard this letter without reading it. I will not insult you with an apology for my transgressions..." The letter went on to ask that the journal and a ring be given to her daughter. "So that's how the ring came to belong to my mother's mother," I said.

"What's going on?" Katrina asked. "Angel said you found something."

I handed the letter to Ida and opened the small black book. The handwritten pages told the story of the last year of my great-grandmother Andrea Baker's life.

It began with her time in Paris with the man she called "Count Cordelier, my beloved Reynaldo," and her "journey through hell," a trip to the Caribbean Island of Jamaica. Her ordeal there took the life of Reynaldo. It continued with her flight to New Orleans, where she made the decision to send the journal, along with her ring, back to England and into the care of the husband she had deserted.

Ida and Katrina both read the journal over my shoulder. All three of us were silently engrossed in the words. "Wow," was all I could say when I had finished reading the journal.

"Yeah, wow," Katrina said.

"Do you know what this means, Judith? We've got

to find the ring!" Ida Mae exclaimed.

"Yeah, Mom, we've got to find the ring," Katrina agreed.

"How?" I asked. "How do we go about it? Marion Webb promised she would try to find the girl's address. I don't know what we can do until she calls." I tried to calm my racing heart.

"But, Mom, that could take days or even weeks!" Katrina shrieked.

"Come on, Judith, let's call her again," Ida urged.

"OK." Secretly glad to have been talked into it, I dialed Marion Webb's number.

"Hi, Marion. This is Judith Barnes. Listen, I'm sorry to bother you over the holiday, but my sister is here with me today and we're really anxious to know if you were able to find any information about the girl who has our mother's ring?"

"Yes, as a matter of fact, Mother is here visiting for a few days, and she has a letter from the girl. I intended to call you tomorrow. I'm glad you called. If you'll hold a minute I'll go get the envelope."

"She's got it," I whispered to Katrina and Ida, who stood next to me eager to hear. They began jumping and giggling like little girls. I couldn't help but laugh at the sight of the twenty-six-year-old and fifty-six-year-old acting like kids again, doing high fives and bumping their hips together. Marion picked up the phone so put my finger to my lips.

"I have it. Are you ready?" she asked. "Her name is Kathy Rosen and her phone number is 823-502-1121. I believe her mother's name is Katherine also. I hope this is helpful."

I thanked her and we hung up the phone. "Let's call here, Mom." Katrina and Ida nodded in agreement.

I dialed the number. "Hello." I could tell the voice on the other end belonged to a young woman.

"Hello, my name is Judith Barnes and I'm trying to get in touch with Kathy Rosen," I said.

"I'm Kathy Rosen," the voice said tentatively.

"That's great. Listen, this may seem like a strange call but, if you could give me a few minutes, I will explain. I need to tell you a story," I said.

"Well, uh, OK I guess."

"A few months ago my husband gave an old bathrobe to the Salvation Army here in Memphis, Tennessee. Inside one of the pockets of that robe was a ring that was left to me by my mother when she died. This ring was passed down from her mother and her mother's mother. This ring is really important to me and my family. We've traced it to a woman from Seattle, Hattie Collins, who gave us your number. Her daughter told us her mother believed the ring would bring good luck and gave it to you—"

"It does," she interrupted. "It does bring good luck."

I paused, not exactly sure what to say next. "Well, I don't know about that, but I do know it has great sentimental value to me and I'm anxious to get it back."

"I don't have it," she said. "I did but I don't have it anymore."

"Where is it?" I shrieked then tried to control my voice. "Where is it?" I asked more calmly.

"I gave it to Marita Esteval. She comes to the rescue mission where I volunteer," the girl answered matter-of-factly.

"Oh my. I really want to find my ring." It was the only thing I could say.

"Marita needs the luck it will bring, so why don't you just leave it alone?" Kathy said. "Marita's pregnant and her mom and dad have thrown her out. She's trying real hard to kick a crack habit and she needs all the luck she can get."

"Well, maybe I don't exactly need the ring, but it belongs to my family and I want to get it back," I answered defensively. "Where can I find Marita?"

"I'm not sure. She comes to the center a couple of times a week for food and vitamins."

"Will you see her? Can you talk to her about the ring?"

"Why don't you leave it? I told you she needs all the luck she can get."

I didn't answer. "If you can get the ring for me, call. Tell the girl I'll pay her for it." I left my number and hung up the phone.

"What happened, Mom? Katrina asked.

"She doesn't have it anymore. She gave it to another girl she met at a rescue mission. She said the girl needed some good luck."

Marion Webb hung up the phone after reading the information to Judith Barnes. She looked down at the envelope. This whole thing with the ring was odd. She wondered about the girl her mom had given it to. Her mother had appeared to be so attached to it.

She was convinced it had brought her good luck. What would make her give it up? She opened the envelope and began to read the letter.

Dear Hattie,

I hope this finds you well. Are you still visiting the garden every day? I guess it's too cold for you to sit outside for very long at a time. I miss talking to you and I wanted to let you know how things are going with me. You helped me so much and I love you for it.

Things are not so bad here. Mom is trying real hard to make up for things. She says she knows she was selfish and she wants us to be friends. She still won't talk about Cal but I believe she's sorry for not taking care of him like she should have. She and I go to a counselor once a week. We go together and we're beginning to talk more every day. You were right about the ring. It does bring good luck.

I'll write again.

Love,

Kathy

Marion folded the letter and returned it to her mother's purse. She pushed open the door to the bedroom where her mother was napping and looked down at her sleeping face. I wish things were different, Mom, she thought. I wish I could make things so you could stay here with me.

"What would you do about her care during the day?" Kevin asked. "Maybe this would be a good time for you to consider quitting work?" He'd been after her to give up her job since the company she worked for had been bought out. Marion didn't care for the new management.

"Maybe, maybe I will," she said.

MARITA
Chapter 11

Marita Esteval left the rescue center and turned down the street toward home, her rooms in the attic over Kelly's Liquor store. The girl from the center—the one who had given her the ring—was right; she needed to quit for the baby's sake. She had to. "The drugs, what will happen to the baby if I keep taking them? I'm not hooked or anything but I need to stop at least for a while," she said out loud to herself.

Marita thought about the ring. Not that she actually believed it really had any special powers to help her. Maybe the girl was right about the baby though. Maybe she could improve the baby's future.

The nurse at the center had told her that no one would adopt a baby who was born addicted to drugs. Marita didn't know about that, but she figured she should try to do the best that she could for it. She didn't want it to end up in an orphanage with no hope of getting out. "Damn it, damn it." She pounded her fist against the rough wall of a building.

She looked across the street to where the blue pawn shop sign blinked. The lights ran along the top edges then down and across the bottom. The blue sparkles seemed to jump off the bottom, at the corner, and then reappear on the top as if by magic. This pattern went on over and over again.

Marita looked down at the ring and, for a moment, she considered what the pawn shop might give her for it. "No more credit," Pablo had said. "You could make some good money with my help but, no, you turn your nose up. Well, that's OK but no more credit," he'd said after Marita had turned down his offer to act as her agent.

"Agent! Yeah, right. Pimp, you mean."

Pablo ignored her answer. "I reserve credit for my regulars." He left her standing outside the door of the building where he lived and conducted his business.

Marita shook away the thought. No, she was going to give the baby a chance. She'd never known her real mother, but it was for sure she would have been better to her than the woman who'd pretended to be. She should have suspected something after Trinna was born. They were so proud of her. Always putting her in front of Marita. Always making Marita give in to whatever Trinna wanted. Not that she disliked Trinna. Actually, she was usually a sweet little girl and, until Marita discovered differently, she had considered her a pretty special sister. For a few minutes she thought about her cousin Elisha, wondering what was happening to her. Had the bone marrow transplant helped her? Thinking about her sister donating bone marrow made Marita remember the day she had discovered that she did not belong in the same family as Trinna. She was not even related to them, any of them.

"We are asking that the girls be tested to see if they are compatible donors for Elisha" Aunt Sondra had said. "The doctors tell us that a bone marrow transplant is Elisha's best chance of survival. They say her cousins are most likely to be compatible."

Both Marita and Trinna immediately agreed to help.

Marita was surprised at her parents' hesitation. "We need a little time to think about all this." Her dad looked toward her mother, who nodded in agreement.

"What's there to think about?" Marita quickly interrupted. "We are family. We have to help."

"That's right." Trinna stood beside Marita.

"We know we're all family but there's a lot to consider," her dad insisted. "Your mother and I have to find out more about all this."

"Please…" Aunt Sondra scooted forward in her chair. "It's safe. The doctors say it's uncomfortable for the donor but it's perfectly safe."

Marita's dad didn't budge. "We understand and we're certainly not refusing to help. We just need to speak to the girls' doctor. That's all."

Aunt Sondra shrugged in resignation. "I understand. I really do." She paused. "Carlos, Maria, I know we are not close. We live so far away and I know our families have never spent time together. I know that our only connection is that Carlos' father and my father are brothers, but I beg you to help Elisha."

After Sondra left, both Marita and Trinna began arguing with their parents. "That's enough," her father finally said. "You girls go on and finish your homework while your mother and I talk about this. We are not going to do anything without taking to Dr. Gillan."

Marita and Trinna reluctantly left the room. When they reached the top of the stairs, Marita ducked into the bathroom. "I'll be there in a minute," she said. As soon as Trinna closed the door to her room, Marita slipped out of the bathroom and tiptoed down the stairs.

"What harm can it do?" her mom argued. "She's underage, the doctor won't give her any of the results. He won't tell her anything. She just simply won't be a match."

"We can't take a chance," Dad answered. "We probably should have told her when she was younger. I'm afraid she'll just resent it now."

"No, no. We can't tell her, not ever. Still, she'll wonder why we won't let her be tested," her mother said.

Marita wondered what her parents could be talking about, but the truth never dawned on her. That would come later, after weeks of arguing with them because they would not allow either she or Trinna to help Elisha.

When Marita did hear the truth, it was not from her mom or her dad but from Trinna. Marita understood a lot of things now. Over the next four years she came to understand more and more. She was basically a captive during the last of those four years. They wouldn't allow her to find her real mother. They wouldn't give her any information except to say that the woman was a drug addict. Well, Marita didn't believe any of it. Finally, it all came down to the day when she was told to change her friends, her habits, and her entire life or leave. She left.

That was six weeks ago. Marita reached the liquor store and looked up at the stairway that led to her apartment. She dreaded the climb, no not the climb. She dreaded the two dingy rooms that waited for her at the top of the stairs. She made herself make the climb. She hung her coat on a peg just inside the door. The apartment had no closets and the rest of her clothes hung around the room on similar pegs. She pulled a sweater from one of these and pulled it on. The room was heated by a radiator, but it worked only part of the time so the room always had a chill.

If only this whole baby thing were over so she could be gone from here and living in warm, sunny California.

Her friend Nina was living there and doing all right. She was eighteen, only a year older than Marita, and she'd told her to come anytime. She said they would room together. Los Angeles must be a pretty wonderful place to live, Marita thought as she pulled her feet up under her body on the tattered, dirty couch. As she thought about Nina and California, she remembered the bus ticket hidden in a plastic bag pushed into the very back of the small freezer compartment of the refrigerator. A bus ticket and six months' rent on this dump, all purchased on the first day she arrived here in Denver. A ticket that would take her far away from this town and her old family once the baby was born. This didn't leave much from the college savings fund she had cleaned out just before being told to leave home. Her dad—no not her dad but the man who had pretended to be her dad—had called her a bad influence. A bad influence. A bad influence on his precious daughter.

Well, OK, so what. She'd taken the money, all of it, who needed it more? She needed it to be able to live and all of them, all of them could go straight to hell. "Hell," now there's a word her dad would have had a fit if he ever heard her say. Dad, what a joke.

She would never see him or any of the other hypocrites again. She would miss Trinna though. No matter, she had to make a clean break and she had a plan. Once she was in California, she'd find her real mother. Marita knew in her heart that everything she'd been told about her was a lie.

Marita pulled her coat down from the peg and began digging in the pockets, where she'd hidden a cookie and an apple from the rescue mission. Since she'd used what little money she had left, after buying the room and the ticket, to buy heroin she had nothing for food so she ate one hot meal at the center every day. But she didn't go back for a second one. If you went back for supper you had to listen to the preacher, and she wanted no part of that. Instead, she always put something in her pocket for later.

Night came and Marita began to sweat. The all too familiar gnawing ache started in her stomach and quickly spread to the rest of her body. Soon it seemed that her gut was twisting and turning inside her body. By the time morning came Marita's resolve was gone. She staggered down the outside stairway and hurried down the street. She left the pawn shop on 27th Street with twenty-five dollars in her pocket. She began running before she reached the end of the block. Twenty-five dollars would buy the fix she needed. She really intended to quit, at least till after the baby was born, but she had never realized it was going to be so hard. The money she got for the ring would get her through today, and then tomorrow she would quit for sure.

LESTER

Chapter 12

Lester Presley sat on a wooden bench in the Portland Greyhound bus terminal and watched as every sort of humanity passed through. After a while the loudspeaker called his bus number, and he moved with the crowd, through the doors, to board the bus that would take him to Corbin, Kentucky. That would leave him a twenty-mile walk to reach Deer Creek, and home. He'd spent the last eighteen months north of Portland, Oregon, working as a logger. When he'd left home for the logging camp, two years earlier, it was the first time he'd been more than fifty miles from Deer Creek in his entire life and, most every day since he'd been away, he'd bothered for the sight of his family and the home he'd left behind in Deer Creek.

The logging work wasn't so bad and the North Country, where the camp was located, was some of the prettiest country he'd ever seen outside of Kentucky. Some of the men complained about the lack of modern conveniences and such, but Lester thought it was quite pleasant. The oil lamps used to light the cabin and the woodstoves used for heat and cooking weren't much different from home. Of course home would include Mama's cooking and Paw's reading of the Good Book.

When darkness came to the camp, poker games

were the usual entertainment. Lester never took part in any of these. Not because he had anything against gambling, but he was opposed to wasting the money he'd sweated blood and tears to earn. No, that money would go into his money belt to be saved toward the time when he would have enough to go back to Deer Creek and buy Silas Morgan's farm.

Today was that day. Inside his money belt was $16,000. The only money he had spent from his stash was fifty dollars for his bus ticket and seventy-five for a ring he'd found in a pawn shop near the bus station. The owner of the pawn shop said the ring was worth much more. Lester didn't really know if he believed that, but then he didn't buy the ring because of its value. He bought the ring because when he saw it he knew he wanted it. It wasn't for a girl. He didn't have one. He just wanted the ring.

Silas and Reba Morgan didn't have any living children. Their only child, Jacob, had been born with what folks called weak lungs. His birth was difficult and left Reba unable to conceive another child. He was three days old and close to death when Silas called Harmon Presley and several other men from his church to come and pray for the boy's healing. For a week Harmon and his fellow believers from the Deer Creek New Life Holiness Church laid hands on the baby and prayed for his life. After a week of hardly any signs of life, the baby opened his eyes and began crying loud and strong. The Lord had answered their prayers.

When Jacob was seven he was stricken with meningitis. Again Harmon Presley and the other believers came to pray over him. They prayed night and day for three days. At the end of those three days, they were physically and emotionally exhausted but this time it was to no avail.

It seemed God had other plans for the boy. "God's will be done. Praise his holy name," Homer said to Silas and Margaret after the boy had breathed his last. The summer sun had gone down and the evening shadows were spreading over the land when Harmon walked out onto the Morgans' front porch. He sat down on the end of an old wooden bench that held a wash basin, a water bucket, and a water dipper. A limp towel hung on a nail in a post near the bench.

Lester followed his father out onto the porch. "Fetch up a pail of water, son. I'm mighty powerful thirsty."

Lester carried the water pail out to the well house and set it down. He lifted the well bucket off the nail and lowered it into the well. After a minute or so the bucket splashed into the water. He let it sink until he could feel the tug of the water telling him the bucket was full.

Lester pulled the chain up, hand over hand, until the bucket cleared the top of the well. He swung it out over the pail and lifted the trigger to release the stream of water. Then he carried the pail back to where his father sat looking out across the yard. "Why?" Lester asked. "Why didn't God answer? I've seen you bring his healin' power down dozens of times. Why didn't God answer this time, Paw?"

Harmon Presley looked across the dipper he was drinking from. "The Lord answered, son. He just said 'no' this time. The Bible says, 'The Lord blesses whom he will.' It don't do to question that." Harmon emptied the water left in the dipper onto the ground, hung the dipper back on the nail, and walked back into the house to face his best friends and their dead child.

Harmon Presley was the founder and preacher of the Deer Creek New Life Holiness Church. Outsiders called them foot washers and snake handlers. Harmon Presley said they were handling serpents in the spirit of the Lord. He said they were following the will of the Almighty, the all-powerful God. He was fond of quoting Mark: Chapter 16, verses 17 and 18 from the King James Bible whenever anyone questioned him about handling the snakes. "And these signs shall follow them that believe: In my name shall they cast out devils: They shall speak with new tongues: They shall take up serpents: And if they drink any deadly thing, it shall not hurt them: They shall lay hands on the sick, and they shall recover."

Lester watched his daddy handle the serpents when the spirit moved him to do so. It was always during the meetings. The other believers sang and shouted and prayed till the spirit came over them. That was when they took the serpents from the box and passed them around. All of this was done so that unbelievers would see the power of god at work. Occasionally someone would take up the serpents without truly being in the spirit and be bitten. When this happened Harmon and the other faithful would lay on hands and pray for God to heal them.

Lester could remember many people being bitten over the years but only one death. That was Ruth Ann Bollins. She'd lifted two rattlesnakes out of the box before the service started last July and had been bitten several times. Lester's daddy said she was filled with self-pride and had picked up the serpents in an attempt to raise herself up in the eyes of men.

"The Lord will not be tempted," he'd proclaimed loudly that day.

Last week when Lester told his dad that he was leaving Deer Creek, he'd expected to hear him rant and rave condemnation upon him, but instead his dad said, "It'll seem powerful strange here without you, son." Then he pulled a well-worn Bible from the inside pocket of his suit coat and placed it into Lester's hands. "This book has always told me my duty plain and clear. I expect it'll do the same for you."

Lester had a farmer's heart. He'd made his daddy's five acres of rocky hillside produce more food in the last two years than Harmon Presley had been able to coax from it in the previous fifteen years. The farm was small and Silas Morgan's farm joined the eastern side of that five acres. Most of Silas's twenty-five acres was prime bottom land, and Lester coveted it.

"Mr. Morgan." Lester found Silas down past the millpond trying to wrestle his half dozen pigs out of the muddy water. They had once again broken through the fence and destroyed a big portion of Margaret's vegetable garden. "I heard you been talking about selling out." Lester bent down to help pull the pigs from the mud.

Silas Morgan didn't answer till the last pig had been shoved onto the bed of his truck and the gate closed. He took a piece of a tobacco plug from his pocket and sliced a corner slug of it off with his pocketknife. He offered the slice to Lester who accepted it and pushed it into his jaw. Silas cut off another slice for himself. "Take a seat, boy." Silas motioned for Lester to sit down beside him on the rise beside the pond. "Reba and me we ain't gettin' any younger and this place is just too much for us nowadays.

Ah've knowed you had your eye on my land for some time, son."

"You know I don't have any money. But you're right about one thing. I'd sure be proud to own this place. This here is some of the finest land that God ever made."

Silas looked out across the pond. "I'd be willing to give you a right good deal. The way I figure it, me and Reba are going be needing the use of the house till we pass on, but the land won't be of much use to us soon. I was thinking to offer the place to you for $12,000 cash money and a guarantee that Reba and me would be able to stay in the house till we die."

Lester couldn't believe the offer. "Why, Mr. Morgan, the place is worth a sight more than that."

"Yeah, well, ah reckon your paw and mama are the closest thing to family as me and Reba will ever see. Neither of us having no living relatives and all." Silas turned his head and spit tobacco juice across the log. "You might not see it as such a good deal when me and Reba are still alive and kicking when you get a hankering to find a wife." Silas laughed.

"Mr. Morgan, I don't know what to say. As much as I want the place, I just can't see how I'd be able to get a hold on that kind of money," Lester said. "As far as you and Ms. Reba are concerned, you don't need to worry about things around the house. I'll be around to help you."

"Ah've been thinkin' some on that money problem. It'll take some sacrifice on your part, but if you're willing?"

"I'm listening," Lester said.

"Ah'd be willing to sign the land over to you with an agreement that'll give you two years to find the money." Silas spoke slowly giving his words time to sink in while chewing and spitting through two fingers he held to his lips. "Now, son, I know thar's no work close by that'll give you that kind of money, but if you want it bad enough you'll find a way." He stood up and spit again before he climbed into the truck and drove away, leaving Lester to think on his offer.

Three weeks later Lester was riding a Greyhound bus across Missouri with the signed agreement in his pocket. He was headed for the logging camps of north Oregon.

Now eighteen months had passed and Lester was again riding the Greyhound bus across America. This time he was going home. He leaned his head back against the seat and remembered his mama's last letter. "Your paw's been more than usual busy since the trouble with them shiners. That family's been a making shine for as long as I can remember, but since them kids was kilt with that shine and all. Well, your paw's been working to stop them. Ah don't have a good feeling about the whole thing but you know how your paw is when he's sure the Lord is talking to him."

Lester wondered what was happening with his paw. He was anxious to get back and try to help him.

ZACK
Chapter 13

The country for fifty miles around Deer Creek had always been dry. The fact that alcohol was illegal did nothing to deter the people who wanted to make, buy, or sell moonshine whiskey. One such man was Zebadiah Gaines. His family had operated a moonshine still, making Kentucky shine, for the past twenty years. They made a good living selling it, and no preacher was going to stop them now. They'd been mostly left alone till those boys from Corbin were killed when they crashed their car and shine whiskey was found inside it. The Bible-thumping snake lovers had been up in arms ever since, and that Preacher Presley was the loudest of them all. Zebadiah's business was suffering badly. The principal cause was that preacher. He had to be stopped.

Zebadiah stood on his front porch talking to his two sons, Gabel and Zachariah. "Since that preacher is so fond of snakes, we'll just make him a present of some real special ones."

Gabel laughed in anticipation.

"Paw, that there's a preacher. A man of God. Surely you don't mean to harm a man of God?" Zachariah said.

"Shet up! Shet up now. You're beginning to sound like your mama. That woman's trying to make a sissy out of you. Earnestine! Earnestine! You come out here.

Now woman!" The door opened and a small woman appeared. She was thin and frail and bent. Her brown hair was pulled back into a bun and wisps of hair fell across her face. "

Earnestine, ah've warned you about filling these boys' heads with that religious nonsense. You've been at it again, ain't you?" He raised his hand to hit her. Zachariah stepped between them and pulled Earnestine out of reach of his father's raised hand.

"Paw, Earnestine ain't done nothing." Zachariah said. "My words are my own."

"Then you'd better watch your words. Ah say what goes around here and ah ain't havin' you or anybody else to question what ah say." Zebadiah turned toward the woman cowering behind Zachariah. "Get back in the house, woman, and this time try an' fix something decent to eat for a change." He grabbed Zachariah's arm and shoved him off the porch.

Earnestine ran back inside the cabin and leaned against the door. A sob escaped her throat. She had been married to Zebadiah Gaines for eight miserable years. He had approached her paw three months after the death of his wife, the boys' mother, and her paw had made arrangements for her to marry him. Earnestine had been twenty years old and well past the decent marrying age.

"You ain't likely to get another offer, Earnestine" her paw said. "Zebadiah says his boys need a maw and he's promised to treat you kindly." Earnestine looked into Zebadiah's face and knew he had lied but, since she had no say so in the matter, she soon found herself married to a man she didn't know and mother to a surly fourteen-year-old and a sweet, unsure eight-year-old. Zebadiah was quick to anger and quicker to use his hand against his sons or Earnestine.

Earnestine took to the younger boy instantly. He was so different from his father and his older brother. She tried to shelter him from his father's angry outbursts and his mean-tempered brother. More often than not this resulted in Earnestine being hit or cursed at. As Zack grew he refused to allow her to protect him, but put himself in her place.

The boys' mother had died from blood poisoning. She scraped her arm on a rusty nail sticking through a board in the new chicken coop. She poured kerosene over it and wrapped it with a piece of fatback to draw out the poison. Still, it festered. Soon the red fingers began to travel up her arm. After two weeks her arm turned black. It was then that Zebadiah traveled down the mountain to get the preacher.

"Preacher Presley, ah want you to come on up the mountain with me. My wife puts a lot of store by your religious talk, and she's been suffering somethin' fierce these past weeks from a festering cut. Ah don't put much faith in divine healin' but she does, so get whatever it takes and come on with me."

Harmon Presley was used to being called out on short notice. "I've got all I need right here." He pulled his Bible out of his coat pocket. "I'll follow you up in my truck."

For the next four days he laid hands on Martha Gaines and prayed. He prayed till he was hoarse and exhausted. In the end Martha succumbed to the pain and fever. Sometime during the last hours of her life, she became lucid enough to call for her husband. She pleaded with him to care for her boys' spiritual needs. "Please Zeb," she begged. "Please give up this feud you have with God and take my boys to church."

Zebadiah promised to honor her wishes but, as soon as she quit breathing, he yelled at Homer Presley. "Get out, preacher! Get back down the mountain and stay away from me and mine. All your praying didn't save her. Now get out of here before ah do something bad."

Homer Presley knew that trying to reason with Zebadiah would be useless, so he headed back down the mountain, leaving Zebadiah and the boys to bury Martha.

It was Earnestine and Zack who usually paid the penalty for Zebadiah's hurt and anger. If any small part of his heart had ever been decent, it was buried in the rocky ground out past the vegetable garden with his wife.

Zack slept little that night. The next morning he tiptoed out of the room he shared with his brother. He knew Earnestine would already be up and about even though it wouldn't be daylight for another three hours. He found her in the kitchen making the day's bread.

"Morning, Zack," she said cheerfully. "My goodness, you're up early. Is something wrong? Have you taken sick, son?" She stopped kneading the dough and looked at him, shuffling from one foot to another.

"No. Ah mean ah'm not sick. It's just..." Zack hung his head.

Earnestine pushed the pan of bread dough to the side of the table and wiped her hands on her apron.

"Something's bothering you, Zack." She pulled him down to the wooden bench they used to sit at the kitchen table. "Tell me what's bothering you, son."

"It's Paw," he croaked, shaking his head in disgust. "He's planning on doing harm to the preacher. He's planning something bad."

"What do you mean bad? What makes you think he's trying to hurt Preacher Presley?"

"He says the preacher is the cause of the troubles he's been having. He says he should'uv taken care of him when Ma died. Ah tried to warn him 'bout causin' harm to a man of God, but you know how he feels about religion and you know how he is when he sets his head."

"Ah know your paw can sound mean sometimes, but ah can't figure him doing harm to that man. Ah expect he was just blowing." Earnestine tried to sound confident.

"He don't just sound mean, Earnestine, he is mean and you know it to be true," Zack snapped. "You know it to be true."

"Now Zack, what do you think he's figuring on doin'?"

"Ah ain't sure. He done some braggin' 'bout special snakes. Ah believe he's 'specting me an' Gabel to help, though."

"Oh, you don't need to be a worryin' 'bout that then, 'cause Preacher Presley ain't skeered of no snake. You can bet on that," Earnestine said. "Everybody knows he's got the power over them snakes."

"Maybe so. Ah just know paw's a fixin' to try an' do something bad to that preacher."

"Well there's nothing we can do 'bout it son, leastwise not till we know something for sure. Now you watch yourself, son."

Because it was almost daylight, Zack pulled on his boots and headed out toward the barn to do the morning milking. He worried about what kind of meanness his paw had planned. He worried he couldn't do anything to stop it from happening. He doubted he'd have the courage to even try.

Being able to care for the animals was the one thing he liked about the farm. Before he began the milking, he mucked out the stalls and put fresh straw in each one. He loved the smell of clean straw and stopped often to lift a handful to his face. He breathed in the sweet smell, letting it fill his nostrils. Once he'd finished stacking fresh hay into the stalls, he went outside to the well to get a bucket of clean water.

He used the water to wash his hands and arms then retrieved the clean pails he'd brought from the house. Zack washed the cows' teats in the water he'd saved from the bucket before he cleaned his hands. The water was ice cold and the cows stamped and mooed in protest. Once he'd cleaned the teats to his satisfaction, he began to massage and pull each one. Warm milk sprayed out in a strong, warm stream, quickly filling the buckets. Once Zach had finished filling the first bucket, he covered it with a lid and went to the next one.

By the time he'd finished milking all three cows, the sun was beginning to peek over the mountain. The light streaming through the barn door was filled with dust particles that danced and twirled in circles till they finally joined with the dirt of the barn floor.

Zack stopped in the barn door and looked out across the mountain. Orange and red fall leaves had covered the mountain, which was dotted, here and there, with the green of pine and cedar trees. Below, the valley was still mostly green. The Deer Creek River began somewhere high up on one of those mountains then twisted and turned its way into the valley, where it passed through the small community of people who called themselves members of the New Life Holiness Church.

Zack remembered the last time he'd walked down the mountain to attend the valley community school. For a while he'd dreamed of graduating from the county high school, the first in his family to do so. His mama had convinced Zebadiah to allow their youngest son to attend the valley school and, for a while after her death, his paw had been disinclined to make him stop. Zack finished the eighth grade and was looking forward to attending the county high school in the fall.

"Zack, boy, your maw would have been right proud to see you with all this education and ah reckon ah'm pleased 'bout it myself, but you're growed up now and it's time you carried your share of the work 'round here. Your brother's been a working beside me now since he turned ten. Course ah admit he's never been one for book learning and such. Still 'n all, ah promised your maw ah'd allow you to keep getting yer schooling and ah've kept that promise free and clear. Yer maw's been dead now four years and ah've honored her wishes as far as ah can see to." His paw spoke as kindly as Zack could ever remember but, kindly or no, he wasn't going to allow him to attend school any longer.

Zack wasn't surprised. As a matter of fact he'd been surprised his paw had allowed him to continue this long.

"Paw, ah was sure hoping to go on over to the high school this fall," Zack said in a last attempt to change his mind. "Ah could be more help to you and Gabel. Ah'll try harder."

"Ah don't wanta hear no more 'bout it," his father snapped. "Ah done said how it's gonna be." His father stalked out of the room, leaving Zack to nurse his disappointment.

Earnestine watched and listened from the kitchen area of the cabin. When Zebadiah left the room, she spoke. "I'm awful sorry, Zack. It ain't right for your paw to make you quit your schoolin' to help him make moonshine."

Zack didn't answer. Instead he followed his paw out of the house and ran across the yard toward the tree line. Tears began to spill from his eyes. He ran until he reached a stand of giant evergreen trees. The boughs draped over the ground, forming a small cave around the tree trunk. Zack crawled underneath one of these boughs and made his way to the trunk. He slumped down onto the thick bed of evergreen needles. "Ah hate him!" he screamed. "It's not fair."

He sobbed out his frustration against his father. After a while he drifted into a deep sleep. When he awoke the sun was straight overhead. He crawled to the edge of the covered ground and pushed his way out through the thick foliage. He dusted off his overalls and walked back toward the house.

As he reached the edge of the yard, he saw Earnestine hanging wet towels out on the clothesline. "You OK, boy?" she asked.

"Yeah, ah reckon so. Might as well be."

"Ah told your paw ah sent you out to gather me some hickory nuts for my baking, so you'd best take this here pail and go on and pick up some afore you head back to the house." She handed Zack a small bucket she had hidden in the basket full of laundry. "Ah've been a watchin' for you a good spell, so you'd best get started."

Zack took the bucket, grateful once again for Earnestine's help. "Ah 'preciate it. Ah'll be back shortly." He hurried back into the trees.

Zack could still feel all the disappointment he'd felt that day, four years earlier.

"Well, lookee what we got here." His brother's voice shattered the morning quiet and jarred Zack out of his daydream. "Still doing a woman's work ah see." His brother motioned with his head toward the buckets of milk. "I declare, Zack boy. If ah didn't know better, ah'd say you was courting Paw's woman, the way you're always doing her chores." Gabel laughed as he walked toward the outside toilet.

Zack tried to dismiss his brother's remark as he carried the milk pails into the kitchen and set them on the table. "Thankee, Zack," Earnestine said, looking up from the fatback she was slicing, with a large butcher knife, to fry for breakfast. "You're purely a good boy."

Still stinging from his brother's remarks, Zack didn't answer. Instead he went back outside. Earnestine watched him through the kitchen window until he disappeared into the barn. She shook her head in worry as she went back to frying breakfast. Zack was scared of what his paw might do to the preacher, and for good reason. She'd seen and felt the results of Zebadiah Gaines's anger over the past eight years.

Zack brought the cows out of the barn and herded them into the field. As he turned back toward the barn door, Gabel came around the corner. "Paw's waitin' for us down by the spring. He said ah was to come and fetch you back with me." Gabel turned and walked toward the barn. "Paw said we was to fetch his snake hook and a couple of empty feed bags. Come in here and help me."

Zack stood frozen in place. He had always been able to manage to get out of going snake hunting with them, but he knew today would be different. It ain't the time of year to milk snakes. Why's paw going out huntin' now?" Zack asked.

Every spring Zebadiah Gaines caught the venomous snakes of Appalachia and milked their venom. He sold the bottles of venom to a company in Knoxville who then sold it to a pharmaceutical company. Gabel had helped with this annual snake milking since he was fourteen.

"Ah didn't ask no questions and you'd best not either," Gabe answered. He gathered up the sacks and snake hook and threw the sacks to Zack. Let's go. Paw's a waitin'."

Zack followed Gabe across the yard and into the trees. The path to the spring was well worn from years of use by generations of Gaineses as they carried the milk and butter to the underground fed spring. The water was icy cold year round and had served as cold storage for the Gaines family for the last hundred years, since the family first settled the mountain.

They soon came to the valley where the spring was located. Zebadiah Gaines stood waiting. "We got what you wanted, Paw," Gabe said. Zebadiah looked at the boys and frowned. He grunted then turned and stepped across the narrow stream of water that overflowed from the spring. He continued walking into the thick underbrush. Gabe and Zack hurried to catch up with him.

For the next half hour Zebadiah walked purposefully, never slowing to check his direction. The path they followed climbed higher up the mountainside then down into a holler. It was easy enough to tell that Zebadiah knew exactly where he was going. He stopped at the base of an outcropping of rocks that extended up thirty feet or so then jutted out over an opening in the mountainside.

Zebadiah spoke for the first time since leaving the spring. "Fetch me the hook, Gabe." Gabe carried the snake hook to his paw.

"Zack, get on over here, boy, and hold one of your sacks open. Gabel, get the pole and move this here rock."

Gabe hurried to a nearby oak tree. He reached up to where the tree forked and pulled out a ten-foot pole. The pole was straight and smooth, and the bark had been peeled off, leaving the wood exposed. About four inches from its end, it forked into two prongs. He ran back to where his paw and Zack waited.

"Zack, boy, now your brother's a gonna raise that there rock, and when he does you're gonna see four or five of the biggest rattlesnakes that ever was. You get your sack ready 'cause ah'm a gonna drop this hoop over the first head that pops up."

Zack's heart was beating so hard he could feel it in his head, drowning out every other sound. The September air was chilly. Earlier, he had wished he had not left his jacket at home, but now he began to sweat. Fear gripped his insides. His father's voice bounced inside his head, competing with the thumping of his heart. "Lord, help me," he prayed silently. "Don't let me shame myself in front of Gabe and Paw again."

Gabe inserted the pole under the rock. Zack saw him begin to raise the rock off the ground. He sucked in his breath. Underneath the rock, a writhing mass of coils moved over and around each other, startled by the rock's movement. He watched the loop from his paw's snake hook fall over one of the heads protruding from the mass. Suddenly one of the long bodies came free from the others. It was lifted into the air, dangling from his father's snake hook.

"Get that sack over here, boy!" Paw yelled.

Zack stood frozen. Paw swung the snake toward him. Its long body whipped against his chest, breaking him loose from his frozen trance.

"Open the sack, boy!" Paw yelled.

Zack quickly began struggling to separate one sack from the other. Just as he began to open the fabric sack, Paw dropped the writhing snake into it. Zack saw the open mouth of the viper before he clumsily closed the top and tied it with a string. The sack moved violently as the snake tried to escape. Zack dropped the sack to the ground.

Gabe began to laugh. "Ah do believe we've scared the little girlie, Paw."

"Shut up. We've got another snake to catch," Paw growled. "Now, boy, you get over here an' hold that sack open. Do you hear?" he hissed at Zack.

Zack opened the remaining sack with trembling hands and stepped slightly closer to his paw. Once the second snake was safely inside the sack, he began to breathe again.

"You boys grab up them sacks and let's get goin'," Zebadiah growled. "Put the pole back, Gabel. We'll need it come spring." He walked away from the rocks still carrying the snake hook.

Gabel leaned toward Zack, who was still trembling, and whispered, "Boo, sissy."

He picked up one of the sacks and started out after his paw. Zack had no choice but to follow. When they reached the house, Zebadiah spoke. "Throw them sacks in the back of the truck and get in. Gabe, you go hang my hook back in the barn and bring me that bottle of gas we fixed last evening out of the shed."

"What are you planning to do with them snakes, Paw?" Zack asked.

"Ah told you, boy. Ah told you ah was gonna give that snake lovin' preacher a present, now didn't ah? You just keep quiet and get in the truck like ah told you to." Zebadiah pointed his finger in Zack's face.

"Paw, you can't harm a man of God. You'll be struck down. You don't mean to do that, do you?" Zack pleaded but his paw didn't answer. "Paw, please you can't mean to harm him?"

"Get in the truck like a man or get in the house like a woman," Paw answered.

Zack stood silently for a moment, allowing his father's words to sink in. "Ah ain't gonna be no party to this," he finally said.

"Then get in the house like ah told you," Paw yelled. "Go on, get outa my sight. You ain't no son of mine."

Zack ran into the house and straight into the room he shared with Gabel. He bumped into Earnestine as he crossed the kitchen, but he didn't stop or explain.

"Zack, son," Earnestine called through the closed door. "What happened? What'd your paw do?"

Zack didn't answer. He wasn't going to involve Earnestine in his fight. Zebadiah Gaines found reason to hit her often enough without adding this. Zack knew she would take his side even knowing the consequences.

He lay across the bed trying to decide what to do, if anything. He should warn the preacher, but he didn't see how he could. Paw would never forgive that. There'd be hell to pay as it was. He thought of all the good reasons why he should just stay out of the whole thing. Suddenly he knew what he had to do. He jumped up and grabbed his extra pair of overalls and his clean shirt off the nail behind the door where Earnestine always hung them. He rolled them up inside the quilt off his bed and tied it with a rope. He pulled on his coat, opened the window, and climbed out. He ran across the yard then slipped into the trees. He ran along the path he'd used when he had been allowed to travel down the mountain to attend the valley school. The path was considerably shorter than the road that ran back and forth across the mountain, along the creek bed.

Zack ran till his lungs were burning in his chest. He tripped and fell again and again. By the time he reached the point where the path joined the road, his overalls were muddy and torn. His face and neck bled from numerous cuts and scratches. He stumbled onto the road and began running down the center of the graveled roadway. By the time he'd covered a mile of road, he was panting and staggering. He saw a man walking along the road's edge, carrying a suitcase, but he didn't pause or speak. He had to get to the preacher before his paw and Gabel did.

"Hold on a minute, son. What's the matter? You look like you've been drug through a briar patch. Here let me help you." Lester Presley ran to where Zack Gaines had stumbled and fallen again.

"Let go of me!" Zack yelled with as much force as his burning lungs would allow. "Ah can't stop. Ah've got to get to the preacher." Zack jerked his arm away from Lester's grasp and tried to stand.

Lester didn't try to force the boy to sit, but he didn't offer him any help to stand either. "Why do you need to find the preacher? What's so important?" he asked. "Let me help you."

"Ah've got to find the preacher. Ah've got to warn him," Zack wheezed, out of breath.

"Listen, son. My name is Lester Presley and the preacher is my paw," Lester said calmly as he took hold of the boy's arm and led him to the side of the road, where he slid to the ground. "Now, tell me what you need to tell the preacher."

"They're gonna harm him. Ah've gotta tell him." Zack's breath was coming easier now.

"Who's gonna hurt him?" Lester asked. "Tell me, son. Who's trying to hurt my paw?"

"Are you really his son?" Zack asked.

"Yeah, I reckon I sure am. Now tell me who's trying to harm him."

"It's my paw and Gabe. Ah'm afraid they may be ahead of me on the road. We've gotta get to the preacher afore it's too late."

"I'll get to him but first I need to know more. Do you know where or how they mean to do it?" Lester was trying hard to keep Zack calm.

"Don't know where but they've got two of the meanest snakes that ever was tied up in a sack. Paw took a bottle of gasoline. Ah figure he's gonna blind the snakes so as to make them real mad. Ah know your paw's a man of God and he handles snakes, but ah don't think he can handle one that's just been blinded with gasoline," Zack said.

Lester tried to slow his breathing to control his panic. "You crawl back under them there trees, boy, and rest." Lester pointed toward a stand of pine trees. "I'll get to the preacher. You stay there till I come back and fetch you." Lester pushed his suitcase under the tree. You watch my bag, boy. I'll be back." Lester started to leave then stopped to ask a question. "Son, does your paw drive a black Dodge pick-up truck with a broken headlight?"

"Yeah, he does. Gabe broke the headlight last month when he knocked down Mr. Silas Morgan's mailbox. Gabe can be mean, same as Paw. Why do you ask?"

"I believe they're ahead of us. A truck like that passed me just before you came stumbling out of the trees. I expect I'd better hurry." Lester began running along the edge of the road. This was Saturday night and he knew his paw would be down at the church, making the building ready for tomorrow's meeting. The road climbed up a hill and, when he reached the top, he could see the community of Deer Creek spread out on both sides of the creek that ran through the valley below.

Once the road crossed the bridge, Lester left it and cut across the field. He'd crossed that way a hundred times while he was growing up. He could reach the church quickly by taking that shortcut. As he topped the last rise, he saw the roof of the church peeking out of the trees. He continued to run down the hill, approaching the church from the back. The black Dodge truck was parked behind the church building. His paw's truck would be in the front. When he reached the first corner of the building, Lester stopped and listened. Voices. He could hear two voices but neither belonged to his paw. He was sure of that. He slid along the wall, keeping his body pressed against the building.

At the corner of the building he slid to the ground and peeked around the corner. His paw's truck was there. He looked underneath the truck and saw two pairs of brogan shoes at the front of the vehicle. Where was his paw?

He stooped lower and peered under the truck again. Was that someone lying on the ground? Lester thought it was most likely his paw. He needed something besides his bare hands. He searched for something he could use as a weapon, and the two men started moving.

"You fetch them sacks 'round here, boy," the older man said.

Lester watched. He tried to think. He couldn't remember if there was anything inside the church building that would help him against the two men. Before he could try to slip into the building, the boy returned and dropped two jute sacks on the ground. Both bags slowly rolled back and forth.

"Fetch the gasoline," the old man ordered and the younger one ran to obey. When he returned, the man spoke again. "Help me load the preacher into the truck. We want him closed up in there with our friends."

Lester recognized Zebadiah Gaines and his son Gabel. He watched as they walked over to where his paw lay unconscious. Lester ran to the truck bed and searched frantically for any kind of weapon. His paw's toolbox was stacked against the truck cab. Lester jerked the lid open and grabbed the first thing his hand touched, a hammer. As he hurried back to the corner of the building, he saw the two dragging his paw toward the truck.

"Paw, do you reckon we oughta fix up the snakes first?" Gabel asked.

"Naw, no need," Zebadiah answered. By this time they had reached the truck and were lifting his paw into the seat.

His paw's body landed hard across the seat. Lester winced when he saw his paw's bloodied face.

"Hand me your knife, boy."

Lester watched from under the truck as the string holding both sacks was cut. Zebadiah held the sacks closed so the snakes couldn't escape. He squatted down and let the sacks rest on the ground. Gabel twisted the cap from the bottle and soaked the sacks with gasoline. Immediately the sacks began to jerk violently. "Quick, boy. Help me hold these."

Lester slipped along beside the truck until he was directly behind Zebadiah. He raised the hammer and brought it down onto Gabel's shoulder. Gabel screamed in pain and twisted around, raising his arms in self-defense. His hand slipped from the sack and it fell to the ground near his feet.

Lester raised the hammer and struck again. This time the young man slumped to the ground. Zebadiah immediately whirled the sack he was holding toward Lester and hit him across his back. Lester felt the coiled body of the rattlesnake through the sack as it slid across his neck. He staggered but quickly recovered and turned to face the man. Lester held the hammer high while the man circled him with the writhing sack in hand. Before either could position himself to attack the other, a terrifying scream filled the air. Both Lester and Zebadiah turned toward the sound.

Gabel's body jerked violently. His arms were held straight out in front of his body. Clamped to his face, its jaws locked onto the boy's temple, was the fat coiled rattlesnake that had been in the sack he'd dropped. The snake was crazed from having been soaked in the gasoline and had attacked the first warm object it encountered. Zebadiah slung his sack away and raced toward his son. He grabbed the snake with his bare hands and pulled. The snake didn't let go. Instead the force of Zebadiah's pull on the snake jerked the boy's face and lifted his head off the ground.

Zebadiah dropped to his knees beside his son, still holding the snake's body. He fought to control the rising panic that erupted from his stomach and spread out through his arms. He knew if he grabbed the snake's neck it would release more deadly venom into his son's body.

Lester ran to his side. "Tell me what to do."

"Hold the snake's body. Ah need my hands free," Zebadiah answered.

Lester quickly took hold of the snake. Zebadiah began to force his fingers into the snake's mouth. "Ah need to force its mouth open." He moved to his son's head. He could tell the boy was unconscious. He prayed he wasn't already dead. With one hand on the top jaw and the other on the bottom, he began to pull. His body strained. Finally, the snake's jaws slowly began to come free of Gabel's face. "Get ready to sling it away when ah get it loose. You'll have to be quick or it'll get you too, boy," Zebadiah said.

Lester didn't have any doubt that it was true. Just as soon as he saw that the snake's head was free, he slung it away with all his strength. He jumped to his feet and ran to help his paw, who was still unconscious in the truck. He pulled the truck door open. His paw lay, unmoving, across the seat. His head and arm hung over the edge like a rag doll.

Lester ran around the front of the truck and opened another door, which was closer to his paw's head. As he passed by Zebadiah Gaines, he saw the old man cradling his son's head in his lap. Lester felt for a pulse in his paw's neck. It was strong and steady. He lifted his paw's head onto the truck seat. When he did his paw groaned. Lester realized he'd been holding his breath when he suddenly released it in a loud swish.

You'll be okay, Paw," Lester whispered, relief flooding his body. "Can you sit? We need to help get that boy to the doctor." Lester waited until his paw's eyes began to flutter open. "Sit still. I'll be right back."

Lester closed the door of the pick-up and raced back

to where Zebadiah sat on the ground holding his son's head. "Help me get him in the truck. He needs to get to the doctor quick."

"Ain't no use." Tears choked Zebadiah's voice. "Ain't no use."

Lester touched the boy's neck, feeling for a pulse. He moved his hand slowly, searching. Just as he was about ready to give up, he felt a slight movement under his fingers. "Wait," he said. "I felt something." He laid his head on the young man's chest and listened for a heartbeat. "He's still alive. We've got to get him to a doctor. Help me lift him."

While Lester and Zebadiah were loading Gabel into the truck bed, Lester's paw climbed down from the cab. He was trembling but otherwise he didn't seem to be badly hurt. "I'll ride back here with him, son. I'll ask the Lord to help. You drive as fast as you can, son." Harmon Presley whispered the last order to Lester.

"You sure, Paw? You OK?" Lester asked.

"I'm sure, son. Now get movin'," his paw answered. Throughout this exchange Zebadiah Gaines sat silent and suspicious.

Lester raced down the road, the truck's wheels flinging gravel. He stole a look into the back of the truck, where Zebadiah Gaines sat holding his son's head. Lester's paw knelt beside him with his head nearly touching the truck bed and his arms stretched across the young man's body. Lester couldn't hear his paw's words, but he knew them by heart. He knew his paw was asking the Lord to send down his healing power for the young man who had, only a few minutes earlier, tried to take his life.

Lester drove past the stand of pine trees where, earlier, he'd left the younger Gaines boy, leaving only a trail of boiling dust. The truck wheels hit the uneven boards of the wooden bridge across the Deer Creek River, causing the truck to bounce violently.

Lester didn't slow down. He knew the young man's life depended on him reaching the doctor within the next few minutes. The town of Corbin was just over the next ridge. Dusk was beginning to fall, and Lester could see light scattered along the street. He pulled the truck into the lot beside the farmer's co-op building, slinging gravel, and slammed on the brakes.

Doctor Ferlin Osgood's office had been located above the farmer's co-op for the last twenty years. He'd had offers to move into the new medical building near the hospital but he'd refused, claiming to be too old to change his old habits. Lester jumped from the truck and ran up the stairs. "Doc, Doc, are you in there?" he yelled. He rattled the doorknob. "We need your help. We've got a snake bite out here, Doc. Open up!"

The door opened and the doctor burst through. His white hair was badly in need of a trim around his ears, but it was well back from his forehead. He was lean, almost gaunt. His white shirt was unbuttoned at the neck and his spectacles were perched precariously on the end of his nose. He raced past Lester and down the stairs. "Let's get him up to my office so I can work," he ordered as soon as he looked down at Gabel. Lester and Zebadiah lifted the unconscious young man and carried him up the stairs as the doctor raced ahead to hold the door open. Harmon Presley, still weak from his ordeal, followed.

"Put him over here." The doctor indicated the

narrow examining table inside the room. Lester and Zebadiah laid the still unconscious young man onto the table while the doctor raced to a white metal cabinet and pulled out vials of medicine and packages of syringes. "Loosen his clothing. What kind of snake was it?"

Lester looked toward Zebadiah. "It was a rattler, Doc. It was a big 'un. Bigger un most." Zebadiah said.

The doctor shoved one bottle after another aside until he settled on the one he was searching for. "How long ago?" he asked while administering a shot directly into the vein in the young man's neck. He didn't pause or look up when Zebadiah answered.

"Twenty minutes or so ah figure."

The doctor began examining the wound on Gabel's face. The area around it was swollen and red. "This isn't good," he said more to himself than to Zebadiah, who was sitting in a chair next to his son's head. The young man was still unconscious but he appeared to be breathing easier. "There's not much more I can do," Dr. Osgood said. "When we get him to the hospital, we can do more." He looked over to where Harmon Presley waited in the doorway. "Come over here, preacher, and let me take a look at your head." While the doctor cleaned and bandaged the cut on the preacher's head, he talked. "This is a pretty bad cut. How'd you get it anyway?" He looked back and forth between Lester and his father.

"Ah fell outside the church building," Harmon answered.

"Hum, how'd you get hooked up with Zebadiah and Gabel anyway? Was it one of your snakes that bit him? I didn't think you kept your pets out where they could harm anyone, preacher." Dr. Osgood said.

"No it wuttin one of my serpents, doctor. Zeb and his boy stopped by the church looking for me. Lester, he just happened to be there. Luck ah reckon."

"Lester, when did you get back?" the doctor asked. "I thought you was working somewhere out in Oregon?"

"I just got in today." Lester wondered why his paw had not been exactly truthful with the doctor. "I'm back to stay," he added looking toward Zebadiah Gaines. "I'll be buying Silas Morgan's farm so I'll be close enough to help Paw out when he needs me."

Lester looked toward Zebadiah, whose eyes were fixed on his son's swollen face, but he seemed not to hear.

Harmon Presley walked to Zebadiah. "Ah'd like to pray for him if you'll allow it." Zebadiah looked up at the preacher then nodded. "Ah'd 'preciate it, preacher."

The ambulance arrived a few minutes later. "Ah'd be grateful if'n you'd consent to come on over to the hospital with my boy," Zebadiah said before climbing into the ambulance with his son. "Ah know ah don't have no right to ask but just the same, ah'm asking."

Harmon Presley spoke without hesitation. "Ah'll go with him." He didn't say anything more before he climbed into the ambulance. Lester watched as the emergency technician closed the door, sealing his father inside with the two men who'd tried to take his life less than an hour earlier. He climbed into his father's truck, intending to follow them to the hospital. That was when he finally remembered the boy he'd left in the trees along the road near Deer Creek. He turned the truck in that direction instead of toward the hospital. He knew the Lord would watch over his paw without any help from him.

Harmon Presley was a big believer in God's answering prayers. He quoted from his Bible often. "Yes I believe he answers our prayers," was his answer anytime he was questioned. Mark 11:22-25 was one of his favorites. "Have faith in God. I tell you the truth, if anyone says to this mountain, 'Go, throw yourself into the sea,' and does not doubt in his heart but believes that what he says will happen, it will be done for him."

Zack Gaines waited under the thick boughs of the trees where Lester had left him. He lay down on the ground using the suitcase as a pillow. He wasn't afraid. He was used to being outside alone, even after dark. He'd walked the trails around his home since he was old enough to walk.

He worried about the preacher and about the young man who had claimed to be the preacher's son. Zack knew how dangerous his paw and Gabel could be, but he'd done all he could to help. It was out of his hands. He pulled his coat tightly around his body trying to get warm. Finally, he took the extra pair of overalls and wrapped them around his legs. After a few moments his heavy eyelids got the best of him and he slept. He didn't see or hear the preacher's truck as it raced past carrying his brother to Doctor Osgood's office. He didn't wake when Lester returned to find him.

"Wake up, son," Lester said softly, shaking the sleeping boy's arm. "Wake up."

Startled out of his sleep, Zack jerked free from Lester's touch. "Where's the preacher? Is he OK? Where's Paw?" he yelled.

"Settle down, boy. The preacher's OK. He's at the

hospital with your paw and Gabel."

"No, you can't leave him alone with Paw and Gabe. They's planning on killin' him," Zack screamed, trying to pull free and escape the confines of the tree shelter.

"Settle down. It's been handled. Your paw and Gabe ain't gonna be bothering anybody anytime soon. Gabe was bit pretty bad. Them snakes your paw had was riled up and mean from the gas. It's a wonder your brother and my paw ain't both dead."

"Gabe? How'd Gabe get bit?"

Lester spoke slowly and calmly to the panicking boy. "Him and your paw had meanness planned for my paw, but I got there in time to stop them. The snakes got loose in the tussle and one latched on to your brother. I guess them snakes didn't know who they was intended to bite."

Zack shook his head then turned to leave.

"Where you goin, boy? What's your hurry?" Lester said tersely. "Just wait a minute. Your paw's been 'specting me to fetch you to the hospital. No need for you to walk."

"No! No! Ah ain't gonna go to no place where paw and Gabe can get hold of me!"

"Why, boy, don't you wanta see if your brother's OK?" Lester asked.

"Ah don't reckon ah know what went on over to the church, but ah know Paw and Gabe went there aimin' to kill your paw and ah know them both good enough to know they ain't likely to forget ah had a hand in stopping 'em. They neither one are likely to let it pass, and ah ain't aimin' to give them the chance to get at me."

Lester looked at the boy. "Oh, OK, maybe you're right. Where are you planning on goin'?"

"Ah don't guess ah rightly know." Zack lowered his head and pushed his fists into the pockets of his overalls. "Ah don't rightly know."

"I'll tell you what," Lester said after considering the boy a moment. "If your willin' to listen maybe I can help." Lester reached for his suitcase, ducked under a tree limb, and walked toward the truck without waiting for Zack to answer. He pitched the suitcase into the truck bed then turned to face the boy. "Come on, boy."

Zack followed slowly. He climbed into the cab of the truck. "Where we goin?" he asked after Lester had pulled the truck onto the graveled road.

"Do you know Silas and Reba Morgan?" Lester asked. Zack shook his head. Well, they've always got an extra bed and plenty to eat. I spent many a night there growing up. My paw used to get on me pretty bad when I'd mess up, so I was always deciding to leave home. As I remember it happened 'bout once a week." Lester laughed. "I'd head on over to the Morgan farm. They'd take me in and feed me. They neither one asked why I was there. They just accepted that I needed them. I was treated like family. I'm powerful fond of them. That's how I know they'll have room for a skinny kid like you." Lester paused for a moment. "You don't look to me like you'll eat too awful much, boy."

Zack laughed uneasily. "Do you really figure they'd be willing to take me in? They don't know me."

"I don't figure that'll matter to Silas and Reba

Morgan. I suspect you've never met anyone quite like them. You don't need to fret 'bout not being welcome. I promise you'll not be a problem."

"Ah don't reckon ah got much choice. Beggars can't be choosers, Earnestine always says."

"Who's Earnestine?" Lester asked.

"Earnestine is Paw's wife."

"Your paw's wife?"

"Yes, sir. Paw married Earnestine after my maw died. She's a mighty good woman. Too good for the likes of my paw."

Lester decided there was more to the boy than he'd first thought. "Tell me about Earnestine."

"Earnestine is young and not a bit like my paw. She's always taking up for me with paw and Gabe. Paw, he's mighty mean to her, 'specially when she stands between him and me."

"Do you remember much about your maw?" Lester asked. "What happened to her?"

"Oh yeah, ah sure do remember her. Ah was seven years old, ah reckon, when she died." She got blood poison. Ah reckon after she died paw never paid me no attention. He ain't never been real carin', but after Maw died he just lost what little heart he had. Him and Gabe, they're just about the same. Ah mean they get along together real good. Paw and Gabe are like two peas in a pod."

Lester believed he was beginning to understand a little about Zack's life and why he felt the way he did about his family. "Tell me about Earnestine. How did she come to marry someone like your paw anyway?"

"Ah reckon ah was too young to know much about it 'cept what she told me. Ah asked her the same thang. She said her paw made the plan. She said he figured her too old to get another offer and he didn't want to get stuck with an old maid."

"I thought you said she was young?" Lester asked.

"Oh, she is all right but ah reckon her paw figured her to be past her prime. She was 'bout twenty. Her paw he figured she'd not get another offer if she refused," Zack said.

"How old is Earnestine now, Zack? She can't be much past twenty-five. You're what, fourteen?" Lester asked.

Ah was fourteen in July. Ah never thought much on it, but ah reckon she's been married to paw 'bout six years. Ah reckon that'd make her 'bout twenty-six or there about."

"That's interesting," Lester said. "Earnestine and Gabe, do they get along?"

"Gracious no. Gabel and Paw they neither one favor Earnestine or me. Paw says she thinks she's better'n him and Gabe. He says she's teaching me to be a sissy with her church talk and her book learnin'," Zack said.

"It sounds to me like Earnestine's been a good mama to you, boy. If she's teachin' you about God she's doing something right," Lester said. "Well. Here we are." The truck had just come to a stop in the Morgan farm driveway. "Wait here for me, boy," Lester said. As he climbed the front steps to the farm house, he was suddenly filled with an overwhelming feeling of pride. This was the farm he'd worked and saved to own and, tucked inside the money belt around his waist, was the $12,000 that would make it happen. He paused for a moment and looked out across the yard. The moon gave barely enough light so he could make out the outline of the barn. He didn't need to see it though. He had it all memorized. He closed his eyes and pictured the field stretching out with the corn standing tall and straight in long, neat rows. He saw cattle grazing along the creek and, closer to the back of the barn, a dozen pigs rutting in the mud-filled pens.

SILAS
Chapter 14

"Why Lester Presley, you're a sight for sore eyes. Don't just stand there, son, come on in here." Reba Morgan's voice startled him out of his daydream. She stood inside the doorway holding the screen door open. "Supper's on the table. You always did have a way 'bout knowing when supper was ready. Get on in here, boy." She turned and yelled into the kitchen, "Silas, get out an extra plate. We've got company."

Lester quickly lifted off his hat. "Good evening, Ms. Reba, I hope I'm not disturbing your evening."

"Land sakes, no. Silas and me was just talking 'bout you yesterday." She took his arm. "You're always welcome here. Silas is gonna be tickled pink to see you, son. Come on in here now."

Lester stepped inside the screen door just as Silas came in from the kitchen. Lester reached out his hand in greeting, but when Silas took it he pulled Lester into an embrace. "You're a sight for sore eyes, son. It sure is good to see you."

Lester was overcome by the warmth of the welcome. For a moment he forgot the boy he'd left waiting outside in the truck. "I'm powerful glad to be back," he said. "I'm sorry to impose on you. I know I just got here but I'm in need of a favor."

"Sure, son," Reba said. "Tell me what you need. If'n we're able we'll be obliged to help you."

"Well it's not exactly for me. There's a boy out in the truck who's a needing a place to stay for a few days. He's Zebadiah Gaines's young 'un if it makes any difference," Lester said.

Silas Morgan spoke without hesitating. "You go fetch him, son. Reba'n me'll set another plate."

Lester didn't move for a moment, not sure whether he should tell the Morgans what had happened.

"Go on now, son. Fetch him in here. He'll think you've done forgot him if you don't hurry." He touched Lester's shoulder. "There'll be time enough for telling whatever's on your mind after the boy's settled."

Lester was relieved and grateful. He'd known the boy would be welcome, but it was still good to hear Silas' words.

Reba got another plate from the cabinet and placed it on the table with a pitcher of milk. She was glad she'd cooked the pot roast for supper. It always seemed such a waste to cook such a big piece of meat for just her and Silas. It'd be good to have young people around the table again. Reba stood looking down at the table. "Ah'll warn up the apple cobbler," she said to herself as she rummaged through the freezer compartment of the refrigerator. "Ah hope Silas didn't eat all that ice cream. No, here it is. Good, ah'll just set it out here on the counter so it is not so hard to dip. Now then, ah'll just slip the cobbler back in the oven so it'll be nice 'n hot by the time we're ready for it."

Silas stood in the kitchen doorway watching his

wife of fifty-one years and smiled. She was always the first in line to help anyone in need. He watched her bustling around the kitchen getting things together to feed the two young men who'd showed up unexpectedly. He missed not having children, but he'd never let on. Not once, in all the years since their son's death, had he let on how much he cared. He knew Reba felt the same way but, like him, she'd never spoken of it.

Silas heard the front door close. "Come in, come in." He extended his hand to the skinny boy standing next to Lester. The boy was scuffed and dirty. His overalls were torn across the legs just above the knees. He held what appeared to be a bundle of clothing protectively under his arm.

Zack rubbed his right palm across the hip of his overalls, in an effort to clean some of the grime away, and raised his hand toward Silas. "Thank you for havin' me, Sir. Ah'll try'n not be much trouble."

"Don't mention it, boy. Ah don't know if Lester told you or not, but we're used to having unexpected company."

"Yes sir, ah reckon he did," Zack said politely.

"Come on in here you all," Reba yelled from the kitchen. "Supper's getting cold."

Silas winked at Zack. "We'd better go on in, boys. Ah've been 'round long enough to know that when Reba says move we'd better move."

Zack and Lester followed Silas into the kitchen. "Ms. Reba, I sure do remember the smells from this kitchen," Lester said. "Is that apple pie?" He sniffed the air.

"It sure is, son," Reba said. "Ah got your favorite

vanilla ice cream to go with it. Now which of you boys is gonna say the blessing?"

Lester looked across the table at Zack. "I reckon I will. I've got more'n most to be thankful for." He bowed his head. "Lord, bless this food. Thank you for everything, my paw, my good luck up in Oregon, my friends Silas and Reba and, Lord, thank you for our newfound friend, Zack Gaines. Amen."

After supper Reba helped Zack to the room where he would sleep. She laid a pair of pajamas from Silas' chest on the foot of the bed.

"These will be a mite big on you, son, but they're clean and they'll be good 'n warm," Reba said softly. "If you'll put your clothes outside the door, ah'll wash 'em up for ye."

"Yes ma'am." Zack was fighting the sleep that tugged at his consciousness. Reba pulled back the quilt and sheet and left the room, closing the door behind her. She stepped inside the room she had shared with Silas for the past fifty years and listened for the door to open and close, letting her know the boy's clothes were on the hall floor.

Inside the kitchen Lester and Silas sat at the table and talked into the night. "What'd you figure Zebadiah Gaines'll do when he figures out the boy's here?" Silas asked.

"I don't much know. I just know Zack don't trust his paw nary a bit. He thinks his paw'll try 'n do something bad to him if he goes back home. I can't rightly say I'm convinced he's right, leastways not anymore. The last time I seen Zebadiah Gaines, he was pretty beat down," Lester said.

"Ah hear what you say, son, but men like Zebadiah Gaines don't change. Leastways that's how ah see it. Ah suspect the boy knows him better'n we do, so ah reckon ah'd be inclined to trust his feelings," Silas said.

"Well, you're probably right. Anyways I gotta get on over to the hospital 'n see if Paw's ready to go home."

"Ah doubt he'll be willin' to leave there till the boy's better," Silas said. "You know your paw ain't gonna leave nobody when they's in need of his prayin'. Your paw's always got to be about the Lord's work."

Lester smiled knowing the old man was speaking true where his paw and the Lord were concerned. He stood and stretched then pulled his coat from the back of the straight back kitchen chair. "You're probably right. In that case I reckon I'll stay with him."

"Does your maw know what's happenin'?" Silas asked.

"I reckon Paw called her from the hospital, but I don't figure he told her much that would worry her," Lester answered. "If you're right 'bout Zebadiah Gaines he might try to harm Paw, so I'll just stay with him, whatever he decides to do."

"Do you want ah should run over to see your maw in the morning?" Silas asked. "If'n your paw and you are gonna be staying at the hospital, ah reckon she'll need to know why." Silas walked to the door with Lester and added, "Ah don't figure Zebadiah'll try and harm your paw again, son. He's the kind of man to feel a big obligation to your paw for his help with Gabel, but ah suspect he's likely to be mad at Zack for telling you 'bout their plans in the first place. He most likely'll figure Zack to be against him. Ah don't see him as very forgiving."

"Tell Maw I'll get there when I can," Lester said. "I hope you're right about Zebadiah and Paw, but I hope you're wrong about Zack. I ain't thinkin' to allow anything to happen to that boy. I owe him Paw's life."

"He'll be safe enough here. You needn't worry 'bout that," Silas said. Lester waved in reply and climbed into the truck.

Silas watched the truck until the taillights disappeared into the line of cedar trees. He touched the bib of his overalls, where he'd stashed the $12,000 Lester had given him earlier in the evening. He and Reba had decided years earlier to leave the farm to Lester when they passed on. As they got older, tending the farm became harder. When they told Harmon Presley what they had planned, he insisted they offer to sell it instead. "He's a real good boy, ah know," Harmon Presley had said, that August morning two years earlier, "but he's still need of some growing up. Ah reckon it won't do him no harm to work for the farm if'n he wants it."

It was soon afterwards that Silas presented his offer to sell the farm to Lester. Now, two years later, Lester was back in Deer Creek and just in time, it seemed.

Silas locked the kitchen door and turned out the lights. He stopped outside the room where Zack was sleeping and listened. The only sound he could hear was the boy's soft snoring. He smiled and turned off the hall light; then, thinking better of it, flipped it back on. The boy might wake up during the night.

Silas saw the light from under the door of the bedroom and knew Reba would be awake. "Probably reading her Bible," he thought.

He had asked her once how many times she'd read

the Bible through. "Why ah reckon ah lost count at ten or so." Since that time he figured she'd read it at least that many times again.

Silas hung his clothes over the chair and climbed into the bed, pulling the quilt up across his chest. "Lester gave me the $12,000. Ah reckon ah'd best run it into Corbin 'n put it in the Mercantile Bank tomorrow. Ah figure ah'll run on over 'n see Elvey Presley while ah'm out an about. She needs to know what's happenin' with Homer and Lester."

"Ah'd go with you 'cept ah figure the boy'll be needin' me here for a few days till he's comfortable with us," Reba said. "Ah ain't leavin' him alone till he's OK."

Silas smiled to himself. He heard the excitement in Reba's voice. She loved being needed.

The next morning when Silas awoke, he could hear Reba in the kitchen cooking breakfast. He realized she was carrying on a conversation with someone and, for a moment, he wondered who could possibly be visiting at that time of the morning. He hurried to get dressed then remembered the boy and slowed his pace. When he came into the kitchen Zack was sitting at the table surrounded by an assortment of bowls and plates filled with food. Silas looked across the table. He saw eggs, gravy, grits, pancakes, biscuits, bacon and four different jars of jelly.

"My, my, don't this look good. Ah don't think ah've ever seen a better looking spread of food and that smell, that smell is makin' my mouth water. Zack, my boy, ah'm shore glad you've come to spend some time with us." Silas laughed and reached for a biscuit. "Yes sir, Zack, ah'm shore glad you're here."

"Hush, Silas." Reba said. You're scarin' the boy with your foolishness."

Zack smiled and ducked his head, embarrassed by the attention.

Silas sat across the table from Zack. Thar's no way even a growin' boy like you can eat all this." He waved his hand across the food. "So ah'll just join you."

"You still goin' by Elvey Presley's this morning?" Reba asked when breakfast was finished and Silas was preparing to leave.

"Yes ah reckon ah am soon as ah finish my business at the bank."

"Well, you be sure'n tell her to call on me if'n she needs anything," Reba said.

"Ah'll tell her. Ah figure ah'll go on over to the hospital and check on Homer an' Lester while ah'm out. Ah'll be home in time for supper, but don't go worryin' 'bout me fore then," Silas said.

Reba nodded and turned back to the sink, where Zack was stacking the dishes from the table. "Thank'ee son, but you don't haf to do that. Ah don't mind cleanin' up the dishes. Do you know 'bout milkin'? Ah could sure use some help with the milkin'. My hands don't work as good as they used to."

"Ah'm good at milkin', ma'am. Ah'm real good at milkin'. Earnestine had two milk cows."

"Earnestine? Who's Earnestine?" Reba asked.

Silas could hear the conversation as he walked out of the house and down the porch steps. He smiled to himself. It was good to hear Reba and the boy talk. That's the way mornings would have sounded if their son had lived. He climbed into the truck, leaving the sounds behind.

Once the money was safely deposited, Silas headed toward the Presley farm. Homer and Elvey had owned the farm next to Silas's since they moved to Deer Creek in 1968. For the first few years, Homer had stayed away from getting to know the locals. Silas and Reba brought a homemade apple pie to welcome the new neighbors, but Homer and Elvey didn't reciprocate. Reba was convinced it was Homer. She sensed a loneliness in Elvey and began stopping by every few days to bring another homemade goodie or a cutting from one of her many plants.

Elvey steadfastly refused to share any personal information with Reba during these visits. She obviously enjoyed Reba's company and soon began serving coffee and sweets she had prepared. Elvey talked about flowers and the best way to clean muddy overalls but never about family. Reba, on the other hand, shared her and Silas's history along with that of every other family in Deer Creek. The only slip in Elvey's resolve was a mention that Homer had served as an Army chaplain in Vietnam before coming to Deer Creek.

The change in their relationship came when Homer fell from the barn's hayloft while pitching hay down for his cattle. The fall broke his spine and his leg, nearly paralyzing him. Silas and the other neighboring farm owners pitched in to do the work while Homer recuperated. Somewhere between the pain of his injuries and the loving care of his neighbors, Homer renewed his relationship with God. His years in Vietnam, watching teenage boys die while the old men who wanted the war sat at home comfortably living their lives, had made him doubt the divine love he had always depended on. And somewhere along the way Homer and Silas became friends. Silas spent part of each day sitting beside Homer's bed. When the weather began to warm, Silas carried Homer to a cot on the front porch where he could watch as his neighbors plowed the fields and planted his crops.

Homer studied the Bible daily, often reading and explaining it to Silas during his visits. Silas, who had never been devotedly religious, began to see his spiritual needs in a different light.

"We ain't had a regular preacher here since Arthur Beason died. That was some, let's see, fourteen or fifteen years ago," Silas commented one day after Homer had been discussing the first book of Corinthians with him. "You know, Homer, Deer Creek could use a regular church. The young 'uns hereabouts are missing out on some needed Bible learnin'."

"What are you getting at, Silas? You're dancing around with me," Homer said.

"Ah was just thinking out loud, that's all. Ah mean it's gonna take a while afore you can do any work 'round here and, well, it seems to me you're probably beholden to most of the folks hereabouts and all. I was just thinking you could maybe do some of that studying down at the church building." Silas had walked to the edge of the porch and stood, with his back to Homer, looking out across the yard. He smiled to himself. The seed had been planted.

Days and weeks passed. The weather changed from mild wet springtime to a hot and humid July. Silas traveled daily to the Presley farm. He did the chores then climbed up the front steps and took his seat in the swing alongside the chair where Homer sat. "Was that Doc Abbot ah saw leavin', Homer?" Silas asked. "Did he have any good news?"

Homer shook his head and groaned. "Pretty much the same. He's saying ah should be able to walk. Ah don't understand him. Don't he think ah'd walk if ah could? Nobody in his right mind would sit here if he could get up. He same as said it's all in my mind."

"Don't you stress out, Homer. It'll come in time. You're gonna walk when your body's ready, not before. Ah was thinking ah'd go into town this evening. Ah don't suppose you'd care to ride with me? Since you got that chair with them wheels, it should be easy enough for you to get back to the truck."

"Ah don't know, Silas. Ah'd not want to be any trouble. Ah appreciate you and the others making this chair for me. It sure has made a difference in getting around the house, but ah ain't sure how it'd work in town."

"Well, you can't find out sittin' here. Let's get goin'."

Silas and Homer had been reminiscing about their childhood and the stories they'd heard from their relatives. Silas had grown up in Kentucky and Homer in Tennessee.

"Ah'll help you get into the truck. If we need anything once we get into town we can get Calvin Lucas to help us out. Ah reckon he'd be pleased to see you out and about."

"Are you sure it won't be no trouble?" Homer said. "Ah reckon it would be good to get out for a spell."

A short time later, while they were on their way into town, Silas asked, "Did ah ever tell you the story 'bout

Calvin Lucas's great-grandma's brother?"

"No, ah don't believe you have but ah suspect you're about to." Homer laughed at his friend. Silas loved to tell stories.

"Well, this was told to me by my paw when ah was just a youngster. Ah don't know if ah ever told you much 'bout my paw. He was always one to believe he could overcome anythin' with the help of God. You've seen people like that ain't you, Homer?"

Homer looked at Silas. "Ah know thar's always a reason for your storytelling, so get on with it. Ah'm a listening."

Silas smiled. "In the spring of 1929 a plague swept through the mountains of Kentucky and Tennessee—"

"Wait a minute. There ain't never been no plague hereabouts, Silas, and you know it." Homer interrupted.

"Of course ah do. It was the influenza but you've gotta remember thar was no penicillin back then so it was a plague as far as everyone knew. Now hush up, Homer, and listen to my story. As ah was saying, no household was spared. By the end of February every household had people dead or dying. By the end of March there was so many people dead or near death that there was not enough healthy people left to bury the dead in proper graves.

"Aunt Gracie Lucas nursed her husband and oldest son through weeks of illness only to see them both die of pneumonia. Only Aunt Gracie and her youngest son, Joseph, was left alive on the small farmhouse located outside of Knoxville, Tennessee. Uncle Luther and Wilson was among the first to die. The whole town turned out for the burying. They was laid to rest in the graveyard located on the family farm. The same one where all the Lucas family members had rested since before the Civil War.

"Hit was such a tragedy. Everybody thought real high of the Lucas family, and everyone was real saddened by their deaths. No one suspected that within the next eight weeks seventy-three of the town's 103 citizens would also fall victim to the sickness that filled its victim's lungs with fluid and smothered the air and the life from their bodies. Sixty of the seventy-three dead had stood over the graves of the plague's first victims, Luther and Wilson Lucas, that day in February.

"But now it was March and most of the town was dead. The sheriff had begun burying the plague victims in mass graves. 'It ain't right, Joseph,' Aunt Gracie complained. 'It ain't decent to be burying people like dogs. That's our friends and neighbors, son. It ain't decent, ah tell you.'

"Gracie Lucas was greatly offended with how the sheriff was handlin' the burying of the people she'd lived around for the last fifty-five years.

"It was March twenty-third and Joseph Lucas's fever had been 106 for the past week. It was almost impossible to rest. He couldn't breathe. His lungs were filling with fluid, leaving very little room for the air he needed to live. His mama, Aunt Gracie, sat by his bed day and night. Joseph could hear her praying when he'd wake from his fever-induced sleep.

"Joseph knew he was dying. Dying wasn't the problem. He knew Jesus had saved him. He knew that when his soul left his earthly body it would travel to where his savior was waiting. Jesus had said, "In my father's house are many mansions. I go to prepare a place for you." Joseph was not afraid to die.

"Leavin' his maw alone was the problem. Leavin' his maw alone to worry 'bout his burying was the problem. His maw had cried and worried over the friends and neighbors gone without a proper burial. Friends gone with no songs sung or prayers prayed.

"Joseph couldn't rest. His maw wasn't strong. Whatever would she do when the life left his body and the sheriff come to take him away? Joseph couldn't rest.

"It was raining. A cold, hard rain had been comin' down steady for two days now. His maw sat in the rockin' chair she had pulled up next to Joseph's bed. He didn't know how long she'd sat there. He knew he'd slept some because sometimes he could hear her singing softly. Then he'd be someplace different. He could see his paw and Will across the way, but they couldn't seem to hear him when he spoke to them. Back and forth, back and forth, he would be in the room with his maw then back again where his paw and Will waited. For days he drifted back and forth. He couldn't rest.

"Joseph looked over to where his maw had drifted off to sleep, her head bent sideways resting against the chair back. Joseph climbed out of bed and walked out of the room.

"He slipped on the boots he'd left sitting beside the kitchen door two weeks earlier. Joseph left the house and walked out into the rain.

"The shovel would be in the shed in back of the barn. Joseph picked a spot next to where his brother Will rested and began to dig. The ground was soft from the rain.

The rain continued to fall throughout the afternoon and Joseph continued to dig. Finally, it looked about right. Not quite six feet deep but it was plenty wide and long. He reckoned it would have to do.

"Joseph carried the shovel back to the shed. No need to leave it out to rust. He left his boots on the porch. They were wet and muddy. His maw was always mighty particular 'bout her kitchen floor.

"Joseph climbed back into the bed and pulled the quilt up around his neck. His clothes were soaked through and through. He looked across to where his maw still slept and he smiled. Joseph Lucas closed his eyes for the last time."

Silas finished the story just as they pulled the truck into the graveled lot in front of the church building. "You don't mind stopping here a minute do you, Homer?" Silas asked after the truck's engine had stopped. "It's my turn to get the building ready for Sunday's service. Ah thought ah'd take care of it while ah was out and about." Silas opened the truck door without waiting for an answer. He walked a few steps away from the truck then turned and walked back to the passenger door. "Why don't you come inside? You can wait where it's cooler."

Homer nodded without speaking. He'd not been inside a church building for five years and the thought of going there now caused a knot to form in his stomach. Silas parked Homer's wheelchair by the altar while he began cleaning the area around the pews. He soon made his way to the front to what had been preacher Arthur Beason's office, leaving Homer alone.

Homer spent the time while Silas was cleaning staring at the altar. He clearly remembered the years he'd spent growing up in a God-fearing family. His father had been an Evangelistic minister, and Homer had known the force of God's will all of his life. He remembered when he first felt the call on his life to preach. He remembered well the years before Vietnam when he knew God was all-powerful and all-loving. He also remembered the years in Vietnam, when he lost sight of his faith.

Homer came back into the room. "Homer, take a look in here." He pointed to the room he'd just left. "Look here at all of preacher Beason's books and papers." He pointed to a desk and shelf showing several coats of paint.

Homer rolled his chair to the doorway and looked inside. He sat for a moment then came back into the church. "Are you 'bout finished here?" He rolled his chair toward the front door of the church.

Silas shook his head and frowned. Homer was his best friend and he wanted badly to help him find his way back to God. He wanted to help Homer revive his calling to preach the gospel. Silas knew in his heart that he had been sent to Deer Creek for just that. He followed Homer to the door. Ah guess ah've done all ah can here. Ah reckon anything more'll be up to the Lord.

As they traveled back to Homer's farm, they made small talk but neither broached the subject that was on both men's minds. Silas helped Homer out of the truck and into the wheelchair. "Ah reckon ah'd best get goin'," he said once his friend was safely back on the porch where he could maneuver the chair." You know Reba can get mean if ah'm late for supper."

Homer smiled at his friend's pretense that Reba was anything but a sweet, caring woman.

"Yeah, ah reckon that's one mean-spirited woman

you got, Silas."

Silas patted his friend's back and turned to leave.

"You're a thinking ah can walk like the doc says, ain't you?" Homer asked, causing Silas to stop midway down the steps. He breathed in deeply but didn't turn or answer. "You're a thinking ah can walk if'n ah had the will. Ah want to walk, Silas. Sittin' in this here chair all day ain't my idea of livin'. Do you think ah like seein' my wife takin' on men's chores 'round here?"

Silas stood still without looking at his friend.

"Silas, ah need to hear your answer. Do you think ah can walk?"

Silas sighed deeply then turned to face his friend. "Ah ain't one to judge another man, Homer. It ain't my place to be a sayin' what you can or can't do, but ah have to tell you ah've considered it might be that you just ain't got no faith in the Lord to heal you. Ah'm a thinking you believe the Lord has forsaken you on account of you forsaking him. It don't work that way, Homer. Ah don't figure a God who'd die for our sins would get his back up and turn away just 'cause we lose our way occasionally. That just don't seem reasonable to me, Homer."

Homer slowly raised his head until he was looking straight into Silas's face. "Ah reckon ah understand your answer, Silas, and you're right about one thang," he said softly. "It ain't your place to be a judging me." Homer turned his chair and wheeled toward the door. "Ah reckon I asked and ah reckon ah got my answer," he said as he passed through the door, leaving Silas alone on the porch.

Silas winced and sighed deeply. Homer's words

hurt but he knew Homer was suffering more than he, so he pushed aside his hurt feelings as he climbed into the truck.

The next day when Silas arrived at the Presley farm, he found Homer sitting in the porch swing with the wheelchair nearby. Silas didn't ask Homer how he managed to get into the swing alone. Instead he sat down in the rocking chair." Calvin and Ellis'll be by this mornin' to plow the field you wanted ready for plantin' tobacco. Floyd Hill is bringin' the plants out later this evening. We should have them in the ground by nightfall." Silas pulled his pipe from the bib of his overalls and lit it. "It looks like the price for top-grade leaves will be good again this year."

The next day when Silas arrived at the Presley farm, Homer was sitting in the rocking chair with the wheelchair several feet away. Still Silas didn't let on that he noticed. This same pattern was repeated, day after day, for the next two weeks till finally one morning when Silas arrived Homer was not on the porch. At first Silas thought to knock on the door. He wondered if something was wrong. Before Silas reached the door, Homer pushed it open and stepped, shaking, onto the porch. He walked to the swing and sat down without speaking. Silas felt a lump begin to form in his throat, and he fought to keep the tears from forming in his eyes. He walked over to where Homer sat and knelt in front of him. "Homer, my friend, thank God. Ah've prayed for this day. Thank God."

Homer touched his friend's shoulder." So have I, my friend. So have I."

Over the next few months, Homer and Elvey Presley

gradually became regular attendees at the Deer Creek church, and by the end of the year Homer had begun to take on the preaching responsibilities. When the members asked him to accept the job on a permanent basis, he was unsure but, after prayer and thought, he decided to accept. Homer Presley was now the full-time preacher. He was paid a small salary as well as being provided with a part of every farmer's crop.

It seemed impossible that thirty-six years had passed, but here they were. Silas remembered every year fondly. Homer Presley was still his best friend. Homer had been there for Silas when Reba had given birth to their only son, and he'd been there when they lost him.

Silas arrived at the Presley farm just as Elvey had just finished hanging a load of sheets out on the line. "Silas, come on in," Elvey said. "Ah've got coffee and apple pie. Come on in. Homer's in town. He's at the hospital with some poor boy who got hisself bit by a rattler."

"That sure sounds good," Silas answered. "Ah know 'bout Homer. Actually that's why ah'm here."

He followed Elvey into the kitchen. "Lester asked me to come by and talk to you."

"Lester, where's Lester? When did you see Lester?" Elvey asked excitedly.

"Calm yourself, Elvey dear. Lester's at the hospital with his paw—"

"At the hospital? How did he get there? He was in Oregon."

"Well, he's back. He asked me to come by and tell you 'bout how him and Homer came to be together at the hospital."

Elvey looked puzzled. She set a saucer with a piece of apple pie down on the table beside Silas's coffee cup and slipped into the chair across from him.

"Mercy, Silas." She clasped her hands together on the tabletop. "Don't keep it to yourself, Silas. Start telling."

EARNESTINE
Chapter 15

It wasn't that her life was so bad. She had things better than some. Zebadiah hardly ever hit her anymore, and he certainly didn't expect anything intimate from her. Then there was the boys. She'd married Zebadiah after his wife had died. Zack was eight and Gabel twelve. She guessed Gabel was just too old to change, but Zack was a sweet, obedient boy with a real desire to learn.

Zebadiah had been awfully mad when he'd discovered she was teaching the boy from the books she'd left at home when she married Zebadiah. He'd made the boy quit going down the mountain to school when he turned ten. That was when she sent for her books and began teaching him at home. Zebadiah hit her then but it didn't matter. She didn't stop. Zack wanted to learn and she wanted to teach him. Zack was turning thirteen and she knew he could walk into a classroom with other thirteen-year-olds and compete. Earnestine was determined to give him what he needed so he could leave this mountain and make a life anywhere he chose. If he chose.

She'd knocked on his door after his paw and Gabel left, but Zack didn't answer. She supposed he was hurt and embarrassed by whatever it was that Zebadiah and Gabel had said to him. He'd never refused to talk to her before. She decided to try again. "Zack... Zack, are you

OK? Listen, your paw and Gabe have left so why don't you come on out and talk to me. You don't have to tell me what went on between you all, but come on out and eat your supper." She paused and waited for an answer, but none came. She knew he'd heard her because she could hear him moving around. *Well, ah guess he's growing and needs a mite more space.* She waited another minute or so outside his door then left him alone.

That was three hours earlier and he'd still not come out of his room. She decided to try again. She knocked on the door. "Zack... Zack, ah've kept your supper warm. Come on out and eat, why don't you?" She waited again. "Zack." She opened the door and looked inside. "Zack." Moonlight flooded the room with light. Zack was not there. The dresser drawer had been left open, and Earnestine searched through his few pieces of clothing. Only one thing appeared to be missing, the pair of clean overalls she'd washed and ironed earlier in the day. *Where could he have gone?*

She walked over to the open window and looked out into the dark. Wherever he'd gone, there was nothing to be done tonight. Besides he was probably out in the barn. He stayed out there some nights when Gabel was deviling him. She would talk to him in the morning. Earnestine blew out the lamp inside the kitchen and went to bed.

The next morning Earnestine cooked Zack's favorite breakfast, fried pork tenderloin and pancakes. She set it on the back of the stove to keep warm, pulled on her sweater, and walked out to the barn. She pushed open the door and stepped inside. "Zack," she called out to him. "Zack, are you in here?" The barn was silent except for the morning noise of the farm animals. Earnestine ran back to the house. Maybe he'd decided to come back inside during the night. She quickly crossed the kitchen and knocked on Zack's door. "Zack! Answer me, son." She pushed open the door and looked inside the empty room.

She thought about Zebadiah and Gabel. They were not home either. They often stayed gone overnight. The moonshine business wasn't conducted in the light of day, so it was not unusual not to see either of them for days at a time. Zebadiah never felt obliged to let Earnestine know where they went or when they would return, but in the six years she had lived there Zack had never gone with his paw and brother nor had he ever left the immediate area of the farm without asking her permission. Earnestine began to feel afraid. She didn't know what to do. She knew the boy did not have any friends down in the valley, so where would he go?

By the time Earnestine had cleaned the kitchen and milked the cows, it was past nine o'clock. She pulled down the can where she kept her small savings and stuffed the few dollars and coins in the pocket of her jacket. She had decided to walk down the mountain and look for the boy. Earnestine found her good shoes in the back closet and pulled them on over her stockings. She started out across the field toward the winding path that was a shortcut down the mountain.

Zack would have taken the trail and not the road. He'd used it every day while he was still allowed to attend school and considered it his path. When she reached the road just outside Deer Creek, she'd seen no sign of Zack along the way. She would find him.

Earnestine traveled the five miles of steep pathway

until she finally stopped and looked both ways up and down the road. Where would the boy have gone? She thought for a moment and then turned toward Deer Creek. As she crossed over the wooden bridge and down into the town, she prayed that God would protect the boy and lead her to wherever he had gone. Earnestine had not been into town in well over a year. She walked along the road that passed between the few businesses but saw no sign of the boy. Finally, she had covered the entire length of the small town twice. Earnestine stopped and looked in all directions. The fall sun was bright and the sky was cloudless. She shaded her eyes with her hand as she looked from one end of Deer Creek to the other. "Ah ain't going to find him this way, Lord," she said out loud. "Please, Lord, where is he?" Earnestine prayed.

The long walk down the mountain and through the town had left her tired and thirsty. She fingered the money inside her jacket pocket. If she remembered correctly, the hardware store had a small counter that sold bologna sandwiches and soft drinks. She turned toward the store deciding that she needed time to think about what to do next. As she climbed the steps leading into the store, she passed Silas Morgan as he was coming out of the door. She had never done more than nod at Silas. He was, after all, from the valley and didn't associate with the likes of Zebadiah Gaines.

Earnestine was about to enter the store when Silas spoke. "Mrs. Gaines? Are you Earnestine Gaines?"

"Yes, ah'm Earnestine Gaines."

"Mrs. Gaines, ah'm Silas Morgan." He held out his hand. "Ah think ah know what brings you into town today. Ah may be able to help."

"Do you know where Zack is?" she asked.

"He's at my farm, Mrs. Gaines. He's there with my wife. Silas climbed back up the steps until he faced Earnestine. "You look tired, Mrs. Gaines. Why don't you come inside and allow me to buy you a soft drink? Ah'll tell you what I know about why Zack is at my house."

"Ah was about to get myself a drink, Mr. Morgan. It's been a mighty long walk this morning. Ah'm able to pay for my own, but thank you."

"Ah didn't mean no offense, ma'am," Silas said. "Ah'll sit a spell with you if you'll allow it. Ah'd like to speak to you 'bout the youngster."

Silas spent the better part of an hour telling Earnestine the story he'd heard from Lester and Zack the night before.

"Ah don't know what ah can say," Earnestine said, shaking her head in disbelief. "Ah knowed Zebadiah and Gabel was apt to do most anything, but ah just never would have guessed they'd harm the preacher." She wrung her hands in worry. "Poor Zack. He's such a sweet boy. Ah just know he's havin' a terrible time with all this. Ah reckon ah'll go on over and speak to him." She stood, picked up her pocketbook, and tucked it under her arm. "Ah hope your missus won't mind my stopping by to see him."

Her good sense told her that she would have to walk the mountain road alone. She was dreadfully afraid of being caught out after dark. Common sense told her it was a foolish fear, but that didn't do much to calm her nerves. She couldn't help it. Whenever she could, she avoided being out after dark. Only her love for Zack had given her the courage to come down the mountain.

Before Earnestine climbed into bed that night, she prayed a prayer of thankfulness for Zack's and Homer Presley's safety as well as for Gabel's life. She packed what was left of Zack's small wardrobe into a paper sack so that it would be ready for Silas to pick up the next morning. She'd told Zack she was sure his paw wouldn't harm him, but in truth she wasn't so sure.

Early the next morning Earnestine was up early and out in the barn milking the cows when she heard a truck in the gravel beside the house. She slowly raised herself from the stool. She rubbed her hands across her waist as she walked toward the open barn door, expecting to see Silas Morgan emerge from the truck. Instead she was met by a man who appeared to be about the same age as she. "Good morning, ma'am," Lester said. "I'm Lester Presley. Silas Morgan asked me to drive up and pick up Zack's things. He said to apologize to you for not coming hisself but he had something come up sudden like."

Earnestine felt wrinkled and grungy as she stood listening to the young man speak. She pushed strands of mouse brown hair back across her head, embarrassed by her unkempt appearance. "Ah wasn't expecting anyone quite this early," she stammered. "Ah was just getting the milkin' done."

"I'm sorry, ma'am. I guess I am a mite early. I stopped by to see how Zack was faring on my way from the hospital, and Silas asked me to come by and get Zack's things. I apologize." Lester seemed embarrassed for coming in unexpectedly and upsetting her. "You're milkin'? Let me do that for you. I ain't done any milkin' in two years. I always enjoyed doing that job while I was growing up." He rushed past Earnestine and entered the barn, rolling up his sleeves. "Where's the washing solution, ma'am?"

Earnestine hurried into the house and began splashing water on her face. She quickly changed into a clean dress, combed her hair, and rushed out into the kitchen. A few moments later she opened the door to allow Lester to carry the milk pails into the kitchen.

"I ain't lost my touch, it seems," Lester said, laughing, while he set the milk pails on the table.

"Thank you, Mr. Presley. Can ah fix you some breakfast?"

"No, no thank you. I need to get goin' if you have Zack's things ready. I was up most of the night sittin' with Paw at the hospital. Gabel is holding on. Paw's been praying for him all night. Paw's a great believer in the healin' power of prayer."

"Ah'm sure your paw is doing all he can and ah'm glad Gabel is alive, but ah can't say I understand you and your paw. After what Zebadiah and that boy done, ah expect you and your paw are bound to have some mighty hard feelings toward them."

"Well, if it was just me I'd most likely be thinking the same as you, but you have to know my paw. He just has nothing but love 'n forgiveness in his body. He'll tell you about how the Lord forgave him and all other men when he died on the cross for our sins so how can we justify not forgivin' our fellow man."

Over the next three weeks, Earnestine visited the Morgan farm three times. Twice Silas traveled up the mountain to fetch her, and once Lester Presley made the trip.

"Paw thinks Zebadiah and Gabel'll be leavin' the hospital in the next day or so," Lester said to Earnestine on the trip back up the mountain.

At first Earnestine didn't seem to hear. Finally, after a few moments of silence, she said, "How is Gabel? Silas said he don't think he'll be normal."

"He's a strange one. I don't reckon I know what normal is where he's concerned. I never talked to him afore he attacked my paw, but I don't know if he was ever normal." Lester saw Earnestine wince out of the corner of his eye. "I'm sorry if I upset you but normal people don't try to kill other people. At least that's how I see it."

"No, no ah'm not upset. Of course what you say is true. God fearin' people don't try to kill other people. Gabel has always been more than willin' to do whatever he thought would please his paw. The Bible says we are to train up a child in the way he should go, and ah reckon Zebadiah trained Gabel to be just like him."

"Well, Paw says Gabel ain't spoke since he come out of the coma. He says Zebadiah has talked to him but the boy acts as if he don't know who Zebadiah is." Lester wanted to make sure Earnestine knew something of what her husband would be bringing home in a few days. He had long since decided that the new Gabel was more dangerous than the old one. "Zebadiah told my paw he thinks the boy'll be OK once he gets home where things are familiar. Paw said the doctor told Zebadiah the boy should be put in an institution for a spell, but Zebadiah wouldn't hear of it."

"Are you saying he's dangerous?" Earnestine asked

softly.

"Well, I don't know but Paw says he's got a wild, almost evil look about his eyes. Gabel won't allow the nurses or doctors to touch him."

"Ah'll pray for both of them," Earnestine said. "God will decide."

Lester hoped she was right. He had great faith in the Lord but doubted the Lord would interfere one way or the other. Still Lester prayed the small, shy woman sitting next to him in the truck would be OK once the boy and his paw returned to their mountain home.

"I bought the Morgan farm, you know," Lester said. "Silas and Reba will live in the house till they die, of course, but the farm's mine now."

Earnestine looked straight ahead, out the window. "That's real good of you to let them stay there. Ah know Silas and Reba think the world of you and, as far as Zack is concerned, well, you're sort of his hero. Ah'm sure grateful he's found a safe place there."

"Zack's safe all right and, if you ever need it, you can be too. It's a big ole house and Reba would welcome you just like she has Zack." Lester had spoken impulsively and suddenly felt embarrassed because of it. "I don't mean to be forward, ma'am," he said. After all Earnestine was a married woman.

Earnestine returned home that evening to await the return of her husband and stepson. Although she tried to pretend otherwise, she was afraid. Gabel had always been sullen and disrespectful to her. As he'd grown older, he'd became more and more like his paw. She dreaded their return. Before going to sleep, she knelt beside her bed and prayed for God to take care of Zack and her newfound friends and then she prayed for herself and her own safety.

Early the next morning Zebadiah and Gabel arrived back home. Gabel stood beside the truck looking around as if he was trying to remember the place. Instead of following his paw into the house, as Zebadiah had told him to do, he turned toward the barn.

Earnestine stepped inside the house and watched through the window. She walked from one room to the other, following Gabel's route as he traveled from the toolshed to the barn then back again.

Zebadiah followed him at a distance. Finally, he seemed to make up his mind about something and abruptly turned toward the house. He swept past where his paw stood and stomped into the kitchen. Once inside the house he went from room to room without speaking or acknowledging either his paw or Earnestine. If either stood too close to his path, he pushed them aside and kept going from room to room. He looked into the room where Earnestine slept and then toward her, and his eyes were cold and without recognition. He went into the room he had shared with Zack. He walked around the room fingering the quilt and the curtains as he passed. He looked out the window toward the line of trees then turned and walked to the chest of drawers. Gabel opened one drawer after another, digging through the contents as if he was looking for something. When he opened the bottom drawer that had held Zack's few belongings, he stopped and looked back toward the bed where Zack had slept. He balled his fist and shoved the door closed then walked through the bedroom door and slammed it shut.

Zebadiah spoke to Earnestine for the first time. "Fix some breakfast, girl. Me and the boy is hungry."

Earnestine rushed to obey.

While she sliced the fatback and rolled the biscuit dough, Earnestine thought back to a time when she'd watched her mother go through these same motions to prepare breakfast for her paw and her eight siblings. A time when she was innocent to the cruel life women like her maw lived. Like the life she now lived.

It was the first day of school and Earnestine was scared, real scared, so scared she was sick to her stomach, but she was also excited. She kept telling herself she had nothing to be afraid of. After all, Maw had been learnin' her letters, countin', and spellin her name and, not only that, Maw had promised her the other kids would like her.

Her sixth birthday had passed three weeks earlier, and Maw had celebrated by making her a cinnamon sugar biscuit. That was real special. Since that day, she had twice helped Maw to load her year-old twin brothers into a makeshift cart and, with Earnestine leading four-year-old Burt and three-year-old Kate, they had made the long trek down the mountainside into town so that she would know her way to school when the time came for her to make the trip alone.

Paw took care of all the town business, so Earnestine had only been off the property one time in her six years. That was when maw took her to a tent revival. She had sat on the edge of her seat listening to Preacher Presley deliver a foot-stompin' sermon and watched in amazement as he played with the rattlers.

Her maw kept sayin' "amen" and "praise the Lord."

Earnestine didn't know what that meant 'ceptin' her maw took to readin' the Bible and singin' gospel songs. She would read the Bible to them at night and, on those many instances when Paw was not home, she would say grace over their supper. That was usually a bowl of watery cabbage or tater soup or sometimes beans.

On the first day of school, Maw wrapped Earnestine's feet in burlap and took the blanket off her own bed and gave it to her. Earnestine shivered and pulled the blanket closer around her shoulders. She had no coat and the mountain air could be cold in early September. Earnestine had been promised she'd get a pair of shoes by Thanksgiving. Then Maw gave her a paper bag with a writin' tablet and a pencil and whispered that it also had a biscuit for dinner. Thus armed, she headed out into a new world.

Earnestine soon reached the end of the narrow path then turned onto the road that would lead her into town and the little schoolhouse where she would spend every possible moment for the next eight years.

The first three years of school were mostly uneventful except for two incidents, both in the second grade. The first was when she was caught eating part of her biscuit before time. Breakfast at home was usually a little cornmeal gravy or a small bowl of oatmeal. In the winter, by the time she'd walked the two and a half miles to school, she'd be starving. The teacher called her a rat picking at her food before time, and the kids teased her mercilessly. "RAT, RAT, Earnestine's a Rat."

The second incident happened when paw was home. Earnestine was last to leave the classroom one day after school because she had to gather up all the chalk and erasers for the teacher. She saw a small comb that someone had left behind lying on a desk. At home everyone shared the same comb. She thought about how nice it would be to have her own and not have to share. Her young mind convinced her that if whoever owned the comb wanted it they would not have left it behind. She took the comb.

That night Earnestine took out her new comb. She turned it over in her hand, admiring its blue color, before she started to comb her hair. She didn't think about her paw. He didn't usually pay much attention to her nightly activities but, for some reason, that night he immediately asked where she got the comb. Earnestine didn't know about lying and so she told her paw about taking it. Needless to say that evening ended with a severe belt-thrashing and her paw saying no young 'un of his would become a thief. The next day, Paw marched her to school himself and made her stand in front of the classroom and tell everyone what she had done.

At recess some of the other kids began to chant, "THIEF, THIEF, RAT THIEF, EARNESTINE'S A RAT THIEF." Words that would never leave her. She ran crying from the cinder-covered playground. Earnestine never again took anything that didn't belong to her.

There was one thing that set Earnestine apart from her classmates. She was smart. She learned quickly and easily. She also had a talent for making up rhymes and putting tunes to them. When the teasing became unbearable, she retreated into her world of making up songs and convinced herself the other kids were jealous of her. This was reinforced by the fact that, even with all the teasing and being called a rat, when the other kids had problems with schoolwork, they came to her for help.

That meant was better than all of them

> I dreamt they was tormentin' me
> Callin' me bad names.
> My mind lit up a candle
> And sent that dream away.

When Earnestine was twelve and in the sixth grade, she had another revelation. By that time, she was the oldest of nine children. There were two sets of twins. She had taken on most of the housework as well as carrying water and chopping wood for heating and cooking. Maw was so busy with the little ones and cooking and Paw seldom came home anymore, so the load fell mostly on Earnestine's shoulders. Even so, she managed to stay at the head of her class in school.

In the tradition of backwoods folks, Earnestine and her classmates were totally dumb when it came to anything sexual. One day her regular teacher was sick with the flu and a substitute was brought in. This new teacher, Miss Forsyth, had been raised in Lexington and she had a much different view as to what should and should not be taught in public schools.

Susie Aikens, one of Earnestine's worst tormenters, kept falling asleep in class. When Miss Forsyth noticed this, she suggested that maybe Susie would be able to stay awake in school if she spent less time with boys in the evening and more time sleeping. Susie complained that what she did at night was not any of Miss Forsyth's business and suggested that she was just jealous because all the young men liked her instead of Miss Forsyth.

Everyone in the classroom gasped and shrank down into their desks expecting Susie to get a trip to the principal's office for a major punishment, but instead Miss Forsyth calmly moved to lean on the front of the desk. Over the next hour she explained about respecting a person's own body and respecting other people's as well. She talked about sex and why it's meant to be part of a successful marriage and not to be used as a way to get more dates than the next girl.

Earnestine never told her maw about the things Miss Forsyth had explained to her class that day in September, but she continued to think a lot about it. She began to consider this thing Miss Forsyth called sex.

Earnestine never thought about why or how her maw continued to have one child after another. She knew about what the farm animals did to produce more animals, but she'd never thought about it as sex. She'd never considered her maw having sex. Now this whole thing was much in Earnestine's mind.

The one-room schoolhouse had a small building about fifty yards behind it. A well-worn path led from the schoolroom door past the cinder-covered play yard to the building. This small building was the school's only outhouse. A wooden sign with "girl" carved on one side and "boy" on the other hung from the inside handle. Whenever one of the girls went inside the building, she turned the sign to read "girl" and hung it on the outside handle. Likewise, when a boy was inside he changed the sign to read "boy." Today Earnestine hung out the "girl" sign when she entered the outhouse. Just as she was about to open the door and leave the building, the handle rattled. Earnestine jumped back quickly. "Who's there?" she yelled.

"How about me and you making some sex, Earnestine?" a voice teased. "What'd you say Earnestine?" The door rattled again.

"Get away from that door, Billy Stringfield! Get away or I'll tell Miss Lawson."

"Now come on, Earnestine. You know you want to. I've seen it in your eyes and the way you push out your breasts when you walk past. No one will know 'cept me and you, Earnestine."

"I'm warnin' you, Billy Stringfield! You get away afore I start yelling."

"The Bible tells you if'un a boy wants to have sex and the girl says no, a big hole opens up in the ground and hellfire and damnation swallow her up."

"The Bible says no such thing! My maw reads me the Bible ever' day and it don't say no such thing. Now you get afore I start yellin' for sure."

Suddenly she heard a shout. "Get away from there, Billy! Leave her alone!" It was Roger Early. He was three years older than Earnestine and no longer attended the school. His sister, Lucinda, was in the class with Earnestine. Lucinda and Roger Early were two of fifteen children. That meant the Early family was even more trash than she was according to Susie Aikens' calculations that the more children in a family, the more trash they were.

"What's it to ya. She ain't nothing but trash."

Earnestine opened the door just in time to see Roger punch Billy in the nose. Blood poured from his nose and onto his shirt. "You ever bother her again, you'll get worse," Roger said. He took Earnestine's arm and led her away.

"You shouldn't oughta done that," Earnestine said as soon as they were away from Billy. "It'll just make him meaner."

"I'll be here when school turns out," Roger said. "I always come for Lucinda and the other kids. I can make sure you get home safe."

Earnestine didn't answer but, from that day until the end of the school year, Roger walked her part of the way home every day. He always stopped just as they reached her paw's farm. At first they walked without talking, but gradually they became friends.

The rest of that school year went better for Earnestine. Some of the kids had begun to accept her, especially since the school principal had started submitting some of her poems and essays to the county newspaper and it was publishing them. Earnestine had hopes of someday hearing them sung on the radio. She planned on going to college someday and learning how to go about doing all that.

None of Earnestine's dreams ever came true. The events of her fourteenth summer put an end to all of them. Her maw was expecting her seventh child and was constantly sick. Days passed with her maw only able to eat dry bread and broth.

Earnestine had to take on more and more of the work around the house, including caring for the other kids. When her maw began having labor pains, Earnestine soon realized that she could not give birth in the normal way.

"I think you'd better fetch the doctor, Earnestine," Maw whispered. Her face was covered with sweat. She grasped the edges of the feather mattress and groaned as another pain wracked her thin, wasted body.

Earnestine sent Burt into town to fetch the doctor. Burt was not especially smart and the idea of walking alone into the midst of the town folk scared him, but Maw was getting weaker and having a really bad time of it so he'd just have to suck it up and go. "It'll be OK, brother. Don't worry. Just pretend me and Maw are with you pushing the cart with Kate on top. You remember how we did that don't you, brother?" Earnestine bundled him into his coat, which was two sizes too small but the only one he had. "Maw's awful sick. You've got to fetch the doctor, brother, or I'm feared she's gonna die for sure. You go on now." With these words Earnestine sent her brother down the mountain.

She was worried. Maw was getting sicker. It was almost midnight and Burt was not back yet. I shouldn't have sent him, I know.

She looked across the yard toward the path where she knew he would travel. After a few moments Earnestine went back into the house. From the corner of the room, she could hear her maw's weak groaning. She walked to the cot where her maw lay drenched in sweat and leaned over her. She touched her arm gently. "Can you hear me, Maw? I have to go fetch Mrs. Potter. I'm afeared to wait any longer, Maw. I'm sorry, Maw. I don't like leavin' you, but I have to get Mrs. Potter. I don't reckon the doctor is comin'."

Earnestine pulled on her ragged sweater and ran from the house. After only a few minutes, she came to a break in the path and stopped. If she took the path on the right it would lead on down the mountain and into town, but the one on the left ran back over the ridge and up into the holler where Zachariah Gaines made his moonshine whiskey. Earnestine hesitated. If she took the path across the holler, she could cross over onto the Potter farm and save twenty minutes. Earnestine knew Zachariah's reputation. She stood for only a moment then plunged down the path that went to the left. As she ran between the trees that lined the barely worn pathway, the bushed swiped her legs and arms leaving scratches she would nurse for weeks afterwards. One deep scratch across her cheek would leave a scar that she would carry for the rest of her life.

Mrs. Potter was known as a midwife of sorts. She'd helped deliver more than a dozen babies for the local women who didn't trust their delivering to regular doctoring. Earnestine was afraid of Zebadiah Gaines. She'd seen him watching her last summer when she was picking blackberries along the property line between his land and her paw's. "What's you doing on my land, girl?" he'd yelled at her. "You get back across that creek, girl, and don't be crossing onto my land again. You hear me, girl?" Earnestine grabbed her pail, ran to the creek, and jumped it without breaking her stride. She hid behind a stand of evergreen trees that grew along the creek and pushed herself tightly against the trunk of one near the edge. She peeked around the tree and watched Zebadiah Gaines as he stood looking across the creek. Finally, he seemed satisfied that she was gone and disappeared into the trees.

Whenever Earnestine began to feel as if she couldn't run any longer, she thought about her maw and why she was crossing Zebadiah Gaines's property. Zebadiah Gaines was a scary man. She'd heard about people who'd crossed onto his land and never come back. She began to run faster, pushing aside the bushes as they slapped her body. When she emerged from the thick trees into the flat pasture, she knew she was finally on the Potter farm. Earnestine pushed herself to run faster. The farm house soon came into view. She ran toward the light that shone from the kitchen window. The light didn't shine on the porch steps, and she stumbled and fell.

The door opened and Mr. Potter was outlined in the doorway. "Who's there?" he asked.

"Who is it?" Martha Potter yelled from the kitchen.

"It's Earnestine. Here, let me help you." He took hold of her arm and helped her to stand.

"It's my maw. The baby's coming, and she's in a bad way. Something's bad, wrong."

Mr. Potter looked at his wife. "I'll drive you," he said. "We'll have to take the buggy so we can get up to the house. I'll hitch it up while you get your coat." He pulled his coat from the rack behind the kitchen door and went toward the barn.

"Let me get my bag. It'll just take a minute. You go on over and warm yerself beside the stove," Martha Potter said. "Your maw'll be fine. You did the right thing coming to get me."

The ride in the buggy with Mr. and Ms. Potter was a first for Earnestine. Any other time it would have been exciting, but not tonight. Tonight Earnestine was too scared for her maw to be excited.

Once Mrs. Potter had examined Earnestine's maw,

she called her away from the other young 'uns. Your maw is having this 'un breech birth," she said.

"What does it mean, breech birth?" Earnestine asked.

"It means the baby is turned the wrong way. The baby is not standing on its head like it orta be to be born. I have to try and turn it but I need your help."

"Is she going to be all right?"

"I won't lie to you, Earnestine. Yer old enough to face the truth. It's likely yer maw won't make it. She's too weak but I reckon maybe we can save the baby," Mrs. Potter said. "Now here, you hold this lantern fer me. I got to be able to see. You hold yer maw's hand. She's already passed out from the weakness but if'un she wakes up, it'll help some knowin' you're here."

Earnestine was too stunned to do anything but follow Mrs. Potter's orders. She held the lantern with one hand and her maw's hand with the other. Her maw's hand was cold and limp inside Earnestine's. Earnestine tried to remember some of the Bible verses her maw had read to her, but she couldn't seem to grab hold of anything except fear. One hour later, at 12:30 a.m., her brother Nathaniel David came into the world. Mrs. Potter delivered him into Earnestine's arms.

Earnestine had witnessed her first birth, not counting the pigs she'd helped deliver last spring and, before daylight, she would witness her maw's death. Nothing she could have ever imagined had prepared her for the changes that were ahead.

Before she died Earnestine's maw roused herself enough to make her promise to take care of her younger brothers and sisters. "You got to do it, Earnestine," Maw begged. "I'm countin' on you. You know yer paw ain't goin' to be of much help."

Paw arrived a day before the burying. Mr. and Mrs. Potter took care of arranging everything. Earnestine didn't know what she would have done if they hadn't. It was all just too much for her now, with her maw gone and eight younger brothers and sisters to care for. Burt weren't no help. He mostly just sat and whittled small animals out of the pieces of wood he gathered near the house. Maw had never let him wander too far so neither did Earnestine.

Paw had taken a job at the mill in Lexington a year earlier when it became clear he could no longer grub out enough to feed the family on his small plot of land. The money he made wasn't much, after paying for his room and board, but it kept them from starving. Now, with his wife gone, he came home less and less often. Every weekend became once a month. Then that became every three or four months. He sent money home and, even though it was barely enough to get by on, Earnestine was glad to get it. The Potters helped them out some and, with what they could sell from the garden and any washing and ironing Earnestine could do, they survived.

Earnestine never went back to school. She was thankful for Roger Early those next two years. He came by often to check on them and help with the gardening and woodcutting. Roger left school when he turned eighteen. By that time Earnestine was sixteen. He joined the Army to become a Ranger. That was his dream. Rangers were respected, and Roger wanted that. He begged Earnestine to marry him before he left, but she refused. She wanted him to get a first taste of the outside world and, besides, she knew the responsibility of raising eight kids when he was hardly more than a kid himself would weigh too heavily on him. It was bad enough she had to give up her own dreams. She would not allow Roger to lose his.

A year later Roger's letters suddenly stopped. At first Earnestine worried he'd found another girl in far-off Vietnam, but soon Lucinda showed up. "He's gone, Earnestine. Roger's been kilt," she blurted out when Earnestine opened the door. Earnestine heard the words somewhere in her consciousness, but they didn't really register. Before she had time to comprehend that Roger was dead, Lucinda fell into her arms sobbing for her brother.

Earnestine comforted Lucinda; then it was time to fix supper. Eight hungry kids didn't leave any time for mourning. Tomorrow there would be beans to break and can for the coming winter. No, Earnestine thought. I sure don't have no time to mourn. Even so, her heart was broken. She'd never really believed he'd come back to her, but she'd thought it would be an exotic woman who took him. Not death. Earnestine had never considered death. After all Roger was young and strong. Not like her maw. Now the last possibility of her dreams coming true was gone, shattered on a battlefield thousands of miles away.

JUST A LITTLE FAITH

When I woke up this morning, the clouds were rolling in.

Storms of life were gathering at my door.

Said a prayer to start my day

All those storm clouds rolled away

Just a little faith will make you strong

And drive away the storm

Faith to keep you going on, faith to live and to grow on

When you are down just have a little faith

Faith that you can hold onto

If you believe that GOD is true

Just a little faith will see you through

Faith will see you through

When the night brings in darkness, worries of the day

Become a raging river in my soul

I whisper, "Lord, please lead me on,

Give me faith and make me strong"

That river soon becomes a gentle stream

Becomes a gentle stream.

    Three years later, on Earnestine's twentieth birthday, August 14th, her paw remarried. He came home to get Earnestine and her brothers and sisters. He brought his new wife with him. Stella was a godsend. The young 'uns loved her. She sang to them, read to them, and laughed with them. Stella encouraged Earnestine to finish her schooling and do some of the things she'd always dreamed of. Stella was educated all the way through high school. She told her that, in Lexington, a person like Earnestine could get books to study and take a test called the G. E. D. This G. E. D. was as good as finishing high school, Stella declared.

Earnestine was ready, but it was not to be. Two weeks after her twentieth birthday and one week before the family was scheduled to move to Lexington, her paw told her that he had made arrangements for her to be married. He had chosen Zebadiah Gaines. "Earnestine," he said. "It ain't right that you are an ole maid. A woman your age should already have three or four young 'uns. 'Sides that, I need to make certain that the young 'uns depend solely on Stella for their mothering."

Earnestine wanted to run. She had heard all about Zebadiah Gaines and his boys, and she wanted no part of it. Zebadiah, however, was already outside with his boys waiting. As they approached the house, Earnestine felt sick to her stomach. How would she get out of this?

Then she saw the younger of Zebadiah's boys. Zack, they called him. He was thin and pale. His clothes had so many holes, she could see through them. Then she saw his eyes. There was something in them. It was as if he was pleading for some sense of belonging and being loved by someone. Earnestine knew that she was, somehow, meant to be this boy's salvation and in some way, when she helped him, he would be hers. "Mama, is this what you meant when you said God would lead me where he intends for me to be?" she whispered.

Earnestine straightened her back and walked outside the cabin door, her bag of clothes in hand.

DAVIS

Chapter 16

Davis followed the street signs through downtown Portland. He had bought a city map at the airport when he leased the car he was driving. The address of the mission where Kathy Rosen had met Marita Esteval was in a seedy part of town. As the appearance of the businesses along the street began to deteriorate, he reached over and checked the locks.

His business trip had taken him to Washington State, and the stopover in Portland had been simple enough to accomplish. He wanted to find the girl who had his wife's ring and buy it back if necessary. He was determined to do whatever it took to retrieve the ring for Judith and Ida Mae. Since the ring had disappeared eight months earlier, they had both been frustrated in their efforts to find it. Judith had always been so settled, so at peace with herself. He could never quite put his finger on the reason. Yeah, she loved working with the youth at church. She thrived when she was busiest, or so it seemed to him. He, on the other hand, was a different matter. He'd made a good living for his family, he had money in the bank, all of the things that made up the American dream, but still something important was missing. Maybe when this was all over with and Judith had the ring back, he'd think more about what he wanted.

"Safe House Mission." He read the sign painted across the side of what appeared to be an old church building. He looked at the address he'd written down after his conversation with Kathy Rosen the day before yesterday. *I guess this is it but I sure wouldn't want to be here after dark.* He parked the rental car in front of the door hoping that leaving it there would deter anyone from stealing it, as a whole or in parts. Davis opened the door to the mission and stepped inside. The inside of the building was not at all what he had expected based on the condition of the outside.

The first thing he noticed was the tile floor. It was shiny without any sign of dirt. Long wooden tables and chairs filled the room, leaving only a walking aisle between them. Each table was covered with a tablecloth, and a vase of flowers was set in the center. As he looked around the room a door opened near the rear.

A young man wearing jeans and a t-shirt came through the door. "Hello, can I help you?" Davis' eye was drawn immediately to the young man's hair. It was styled in spikes reaching one to two inches from his otherwise handsome head. It wasn't the spikes that caught Davis' eye so much as it was the color, bright flaming orange.

"I, uh, I don't know. I, uh, I'm looking for one of your associates," Davis stammered, unable to take his eyes off the orange hair.

"Are you a cop?" the young man asked.

"No, no, I'm not a policeman. I'm looking for Kathy Rosen. I spoke to her on the phone and she said she works here on Tuesday and Thursday."

The young man stood looking at him for a moment. Davis offered his hand. "I'm Davis Barnes." Still the boy didn't answer. Finally Davis asked, "Kathy Rosen, is she here?"

The boy continued to stare at Davis for a moment then turned back to the door. "Wait here."

A minute or so later the door opened again, but this time a young girl came through. She was short, probably no more than five feet tall. Her dark hair was loose but covered by a net. The net reminded Davis of the ones he'd seen worn by the lunchroom workers, oh so many years ago, when he'd attended public school. The girl didn't appear to be wearing makeup. Her complexion was darker than his own daughter's, and her fluid eyes were dark brown, almost black. "I'm Kathy Rosen. Mr. Barnes, I hope you've not made a long trip for nothing."

"Well, I was close by, in Seattle, and the stop here wasn't much of a problem, and besides the ring it means so much to my wife and her family that I needed to try to find it."

"Kathy," the orange-haired guy said. "Is everything cool?"

Kathy turned back to face the boy. "Everything's fine, thanks." She turned back to face Davis. "That's Robert. I can't tell you much more than I've already told your wife. The girl came into the mission every week. She was pregnant and really down and out. I thought I could help her. I thought the ring would bring her luck. Maybe it has. She's not been back in weeks."

"Do you know where she lives?" Davis asked.

"No, I don't know anything except her name. There are a few Mexicans who come in every day. Maybe one of them can help you. If you want to hang around, make yourself at home."

Robert interjected himself into the conversation. "Are you looking for Marita?"

"Do you know where she lives, Robert?" Kathy asked.

"Maybe, maybe I can find her. You wait here with Kathy. I'll be back in an hour or so." He started toward the door but stopped and turned back. "We were peeling potatoes. Since I'm leaving, I guess you'll have to take my place." The young man smiled and disappeared through the door and into the street.

Davis looked at Kathy, somewhat surprised.

"You don't have to help but come on back and get some coffee while you wait," she said.

For the next hour and a half, Davis didn't peel potatoes but he did cut up chicken to get it ready to fry. "We buy the whole hen," Burton Hines explained while teaching Davis the proper way to cut up a whole chicken for frying." The whole hens are cheaper and that means we can feed a few more or maybe some can get second helpings. It takes a little extra work but we have to stretch our dollars, you know. Sometimes the hens are a little tough, but our customers don't complain. They're just happy to get the meal."

"How long have you been volunteering here?" Davis asked. They were about halfway through the two hundred pounds of chicken, and Davis was trying to get the hang of cutting apart the thigh from the leg.

"Volunteering! I ain't volunteering. I live here at the mission and cooking is my contribution. I've been cooking here for six years now. I came in off the street one day in January, six years ago and I just never left."

"Oh, I see." Davis didn't know what else to say. "You're a former client then."

"Ain't nothing former about it. I'm an alcoholic and drug addict. I served two stints in Vietnam. I was shot up some during my second time there, and they sent me back to the good ole US of A and fed me morphine for six months.

"I guess I grew a little too fond of it so they put me in a rehab center. I quit taking the morphine but then I began to grow fond of Early Times bourbon whiskey. I lived on the street. I was off and on the morphine and the whiskey. I visited most every rehab center in this part of the country till I came here six years ago. I'm still here and I ain't leaving except when the good Lord sends for me."

Davis stood silently listening to the story of Burton Hines's life. As he listened he felt guilty for his relatively safe and secure life, and he didn't know what to say.

Suddenly his mama's face came to mind and he remembered her deep, unshakeable faith in God. "I, well, I guess that says it all," he finally said. "If you're happy here then I say good for you."

"Don't mind me, Mr. Barnes. I get a little tired of people coming in here and giving me advice about starting over out there in the world, where I can make a contribution to society. Well, I made my contribution. I made it in the rice fields of Vietnam. I made it without thanks or appreciation. I'm here now and this is where I'm staying so if you have a mind to lecture, don't," Burton said matter-of-factly, never stopping his chicken cutting.

Kathy Rosen stood by, pretending not to hear the conversation, but she was curious about what Davis was thinking. He seems like a decent, caring person. She watched him work alongside Burton in the mess of chicken pieces. "Are there any missions like this one where you come from, Mr. Barnes?" she asked.

"No, well, I don't really know. I never paid much attention."

"Most of the people who come here are regulars. You know what I mean. They're the same ones day in and out, but occasionally someone comes through and we're able to make a difference in their lives," Kathy said in response to one of the questions Davis asked over the next two hours, while waiting for the Robert to return.

"This is the address," Robert said when he came into the mission kitchen. "I don't think it'll do you much good to go there though. These people won't talk to you."

"Thank you," Davis answered. "I hope you're wrong, though. It's really important I find out about the ring."

Kathy whispered something to the boy, and he shook his head. She whispered again, this time taking hold of his arm. He looked at her then shrugged in acceptance. "I'll take you over there. Do you speak Spanish?"

"No, actually, I don't. I sure do appreciate your help, son." Davis washed his hands and arms in the nearby sink and, after saying goodbye to Kathy and Burton, followed Robert out into the street.

"My car is parked out front. We can drive there, can't we?" he asked.

They drove along the same streets Davis had traveled trying to find the mission. They passed many apartment buildings, all of them old and badly in need of repair. Following Robert's directions, he stopped in an alley alongside one of these.

"Tell me what you're looking for and let me do the talking," Robert said before they left the car. "Some of these people don't speak English—most do, but they pretend not to understand."

Davis explained all he could about the ring while he followed the boy into the building and up three flights of stairs. I should be worried about my safety, he thought, but I'm not.

Robert stopped in front of a door and knocked. The door had been painted white at some time or another, but now it was cracked, chipped and dirty, more brown than white.

The door was opened by a very pregnant girl. Davis guessed she was no more than seventeen years old.

"Hola. Como esta?" Robert said. "Mi amigo no hablo espanol por favor." He pointed to his finger to indicate a ring since he did not know the word in Spanish. "Ring, por favor, ring."

"No, I didn't take the ring. The girl at the mission gave it to me," the girl answered defensively.

She tried to push the door closed.

"Peace, my friend here ain't looking to cause you any trouble. He just needs to find the ring. It's like a family thing, if you know what I mean," Robert said. "He's willing to buy the ring."

The girl looked out through the crack in the door. "How much?"

Robert turned toward Davis. "How much?"

Davis was caught off guard. When he had offered to pay for the ring, he'd had no thought of how much. "I don't know," he stammered. "A hundred dollars, I suppose."

"Go away," the girl said. "I'll bring the ring to the mission later today." She closed the door and Davis heard the lock snap. He looked at his watch. He'd have to take a later flight. "OK, I'll wait at the mission. I suppose Burton will find me something to do."

"You can count on that," Robert answered. "He don't cut anybody no slack."

Davis waited all afternoon and into the evening. He helped prepare and serve the evening meal. Still the girl didn't show. Finally, when it was getting close to 9:00 p.m., he looked at his watch.

"She probably won't show," Robert said. "If you want me to, I'll go back over there in the morning and see what I can find."

"Thank you. I'd really appreciate it. I hate to be a problem for you, but do you think you could direct me to a hotel where I can spend the night?"

Burton had just come into the room. "There ain't no safe hotel around here," he said. "We got beds here. They're clean and safe. There's no room service but you're welcome to stay. I guess you cut up enough chicken to pay for a night's lodging." Burton laughed.

"Well. I, uh, thank you but what about my car?"

Davis asked.

Finally, after discussing the options for a few minutes, they decided Robert would drive the car to his parents' home then bring it back in the morning. Kathy would call her mom and tell her she wouldn't need a ride; then she would drive Robert's Volkswagen.

Davis and Burton talked into the night. Davis was left with a new insight into a lifestyle he had never known existed. He quietly thanked God for his life but vowed to make a change. He vowed to get involved when he returned home.

Davis remembered his mama's words as clearly as if it were yesterday. "God made you for a purpose, son. I don't know what it is and, from the way you're living, I don't think you know either but, make no mistake, you have one. All this rushing about won't satisfy you no matter what you think. You won't have no peace till you find out what it is God has planned for you."

The next morning Davis helped with breakfast. At about ten o'clock Robert arrived with his car. From force of habit, Davis looked at his watch.

"You thought I might not show up, huh?" Robert asked. He didn't wait for a response. He probably didn't really want one. He probably just wanted to shock this new outsider. "I talked to the girl. She pawned the ring a few days after she got it."

She went out yesterday to try to get it back for the hundred dollars, but it was gone. Do you want to go to the pawn shop?"

"That would be great. Let me thank Burton and I'll be ready," Davis answered.

The pawn shop was located on the outskirts of the area where the mission stood. By the time they reached it, the buildings were beginning to look almost prosperous.

"Can I help you?" the man behind the counter asked. He looked Robert over, then looked at Davis and finally decided they looked prosperous enough to deserve his attention.

"I hope you can. My name is Davis Barnes and I'm looking for a ring."

"Well, you came to the right place. I've got all kinds of rings," the pawn shop owner gushed while he began pulling rings from inside the glass case. "I've got diamonds, I've got rubies and pearls. I've got silver rings and I've got gold rings. You name it and I've got it—"

"I hope you're right," Davis interrupted. "I'm looking for one ring in particular. It has a black stone set in a gold band."

"Black, black, I don't believe I've got anything in black but let me show you this nice pearl or maybe this ruby is more to your liking."

"Thank you, but I'm looking for a ring that belongs to my wife. It was pawned to you about three months ago."

"Black, let's see. Black, yeah I do seem to remember a black ring. Kinda ugly if I remember right. It was a pretty good imitation stone, though." He began thumbing through a book. "Let's see, I can remember it. I sold it to a young man from the South as I recall." He continued looking through the book.

"Here, here it is. I never forget a face. I've got one of those phogetic memories," he said, mispronouncing the word badly. "The boy was young, about twenty-five or so. I remember his accent. Here's his name and address. Don't know why he wrote his address. I only asked for his name." He handed the book to Davis, smiling proudly. "No phone number, just an address." The pawn shop owner laughed. "I guess Ma Bell ain't made it to Kentucky yet."

Davis copied the address onto his notepad. "Thank you so much." He shook the pawn shop owner's hand. "This means a lot to me."

"Are you sure I can't interest you in one of these rings? I'm sure your wife would like any of them. I'll bet your son there would like one of these CD players." The owner pointed to a shelf that held a dozen CD players and televisions.

"No, no thank you, but please take this for your trouble." Davis slipped a twenty-dollar bill into the man's hand.

Davis delivered Robert back to the mission. "I appreciate your help." He parked in front of the mission and followed Robert inside.

"Well, did you have any luck?" Burton asked from across the room, where he was busy putting tablecloths on the tables along with vases of flowers.

"Yes, we did. In fact, we have an address. I don't know how to thank all of you for your help," Davis answered.

"We don't expect any thanks. Just pass the favor along to someone else," Burton said.

"Well I can certainly do that." Davis walked across the room to where Burton was still arranging vases of flowers. "My experience here has been a real eye opener for me and I appreciate your honesty. Thank you for sharing your story with me."

Burton nodded but continued working. "Do you know why I put cloth table coverings and flowers on these tables? I mean this ain't no restaurant and these people sure ain't paying customers, now are they?"

"I don't know. I guess it does seem strange. A lot of work for nothing."

"You just said it all. A lot of work for nothing," Burton said. "Well, I want these people to know they're not nothing. I want them to know they're important enough to deserve a real cloth on the table just like rich people. If you think people down on their luck are nothings, then you'll never reach any of them. If you know the scriptures, then you know Jesus of Nazareth chose nothing people to spread his word. He didn't chose the rich or the important ones. No, he chose the nothings like me." Burton stopped working and looked directly at Davis.

Davis left the mission feeling confused and ashamed of how little he knew about the people in his hometown who needed help. He'd been proud of helping out the day before. He'd felt smug and satisfied to have worked beside Burton in the kitchen. He was leaving with what he'd come to find out about the ring, but he was also leaving with a lot of unanswered questions about himself and his life. Something in Burton's words had shaken a little of his self-satisfied life.

Not wanting to face his selfishness, he instead chose to brush it off as not his concern. "Those kinds of people are not my problem," he said out loud. "There's plenty of agencies to take care of it. I pay taxes and give money to the church for that," he said. Still the nagging feeling of being called to do more tugged at him as he drove the rental car to the airport. *I'll be OK once I get home. I'll give Judith this address and maybe offer to go with her to find the young man.* He tried to take his mind off the restless feelings he had.

Feelings he'd left behind when he left Piney, Tennessee, thirty years earlier.

PAID IN FULL
Chapter 17

Earnestine wasn't anxious for Zebadiah to begin asking questions about Zack's whereabouts. She wasn't going to tell a lie but, on the other hand, she had no intention of helping him find Zack. She finished the breakfast Zebadiah had ordered and went out onto the porch to tell him it was ready. She watched as Zebadiah followed Gabel from the shed to the barn and back again. There was something strange about the boy. He paid no attention to his father while he walked back and forth between the barn and the shed as if he was on a mission to find some valuable artifact.

His father, on the other hand, seemed almost fearful of the boy and allowed him a wide berth in his movements. Earnestine called out to Zebadiah, telling him the meal was ready. She hurried into her bedroom, where she could see the two men through the windows.

"Son, why don't you come on into the kitchen and eat," Zebadiah said. Gabel ignored his father as he began removing tools from the shed and carrying them to the barn. "Gabel, ah said the food is ready on the table. We need to go in and eat while it's still hot."

Still Gabel did not stop or answer. After a few minutes Earnestine saw Zebadiah leave the yard and go into the house alone. Since her bedroom was built off the kitchen, she could hear Zebadiah pull a chair out from the table. She heard the clink of the spoon as he filled his plate. Earnestine moved back to the window and began watching Gabel as he carried the last of the tools from the shed and into the barn. "Ah wonder what you're up to," she said to herself. Suddenly Gabel turned from what he was doing and looked toward the window where Earnestine stood watching. She jumped back, trying to get away from the open curtain, her heart racing. Gabel's eyes seemed to penetrate the curtain where Earnestine stood stiff and still. His eyes raked across to the side of the house then returned to peer into the window where Earnestine stood hidden. Although she could no longer see him, she knew he continued to stare into the window. Something about his eyes was different from the sullen, disrespectful boy of three weeks ago. Earnestine could hear movement just outside the window and she knew he had walked over to the house. She pressed her body back against the wall, trying to sink into the boards.

Fear gripped Earnestine's chest. Her stomach pulled tight into a knot. She waited until she thought the boy was no longer watching then pulled the curtain closed across the window.

She pressed her ear against the door and listened. When she didn't hear any noise from the kitchen, she slowly opened the door and looked inside. Zebadiah was gone. The food was still sitting on the table along with his used plate. Earnestine ran across the room and opened a drawer. She fumbled through the utensils till her hand rested on a wooden handle. She kept her eyes riveted on the door leading to the outside, looking down only long enough to identify the butcher knife. She jerked it free of the drawer and tucked it inside the folds of her skirt. Then she ran back into her room and slammed the door shut.

There was no lock. She looked around the sparsely furnished room for something to brace the door with. Finally she raced back into the kitchen and grabbed a chair from beneath the table. Once back inside her room, she pushed the chair under the knob and shoved it until it was wedged tight.

She retrieved the knife from where she had tossed it and slumped down to the edge of the bed, the knife held firmly in both hands. The snake venom had done something to the boy. Gabel was changed. The eyes she had seen peering through her window had been filled with something wild, something evil. Earnestine was scared. She'd never been afraid of Zebadiah or Gabel. Both were hateful and mean, but this had never really caused her to feel fear. Not so today. Today Gabel had the look of hate, dark menacing hate, and Earnestine was afraid. She was glad Zack was safe at the Morgan farm.

Earnestine stayed locked in the room all afternoon and into the dark of night. She didn't clean the dishes or cook supper. She expected a command from Zebadiah, demanding his evening meal, but it never came. As far as she could tell, no one else was in the house.

Finally, sometime after darkness had fallen, she drifted into sleep. Although she lay across the bed, she never let go of the knife. When she awoke sometime during the night, her full bladder was painfully in need of being emptied. She leaned against the door and listened, trying to decide if anyone was in the kitchen. Zebadiah had installed an inside toilet two years earlier, but in order to reach it she would have to cross the kitchen. When she didn't hear any noise, she removed the chair and slowly opened the door. Earnestine held the knife tightly as she looked out, first left then right. The moonlight streaming through the window allowed her to see fairly well. When she was satisfied that the room was empty, she stepped through the doorway. Instantly her foot struck something solid. She jumped back and looked at the floor, holding the knife in front of her body.

There on the floor, stretched out across her doorway, was Zebadiah. He sat up suddenly alerted by her kick in his back. "Earnestine, is that you girl?" He pulled back, suddenly seeing the knife in her hand. "Don't be afeared of me, girl. Ah ain't here to harm you."

"What are you doing here, Zeb? What are you a doin in front of my door?" she asked, not letting go of the knife.

Zebadiah didn't answer the question. "Where you a goin'?"

"To the toilet. Ah asked you what you're doin' here, Zeb."

"Get on in there and get your business done then get back to your room."

She stepped around him and hurried to the toilet. When she came out and went back into her room, Zebadiah spoke. "Put that chair back agin the door, girl."

Earnestine knew that, for some reason, he was afraid for her. Although it was unlike him to put himself out to protect her or anybody else, she didn't question it. She was grateful. Try as she might, Earnestine was not able to sleep again. She saw the first light of morning underneath the doorway and around the edges of the curtains.

She knew morning had arrived. Earnestine dressed then removed the chair from underneath the doorknob and slowly opened the door. Earlier, she had stitched a pouch in the folds of her skirt and placed the knife inside. Zebadiah was gone from the kitchen. After she cleaned the remnants of yesterday's supper from the table, she set out to fix breakfast. Two buckets of milk sat on the table. Zebadiah had never milked the cows, not even once, in the six years she'd been married to him. He considered that, along with caring for the chickens and tending the garden, as woman's work. Zack had been her only helper.

Zebadiah's oddly protective gestures had touched her, and she set out to make his morning meal with a little extra care, making sure the biscuits were just right and the eggs cooked without breaking any yolks. Once she was finished, she stepped out onto the porch and pulled the bell rope that would summon him to come and eat.

Earnestine busied herself around the kitchen waiting for Zebadiah to appear. She wanted to acknowledge his unexpected kindness. An hour passed, then two, with no sign of either Zebadiah or Gabel. She went into Zack and Gabel's room. The beds were untouched and she knew that, wherever Gabel had spent the night, it hadn't been in there.

She finally cleaned the untouched breakfast from the table. She wrapped the biscuits and put them back in the oven to keep warm. She walked out onto the porch and looked across the yard. There was no sign of either

Zebadiah or Gabel. Sometime around noon she decided to walk out to the barn and look inside.

The tools from the shed were piled in the middle of the floor. A sudden chill ran down her back making the hairs on her neck rise. She ran back to the house, anxious to be back in the safety of her kitchen. It was past time for Zebadiah to want his dinner, so she fried pork chops and potatoes to go with the biscuits.

Earnestine pulled her rocking chair next to the window where the sunlight was brightest and lifted her unfinished quilt top onto her lap. She began sewing together the scraps of fabric she'd cut into shapes that would make a butterfly. She sewed with tiny, tight, delicate stitches. Quilting always made her think about her mama. Quilting was the one chore her mama had loved, and she had passed that love along to Earnestine, teaching her to imagine the picture she wanted to make and draw the pattern on a brown paper bag she'd torn apart and smoothed out flat with her iron. Her mama had also taught her to use scraps of fabric to transform the patterns into the beautiful quilts that graced the walls and beds of her home.

While Earnestine worked making the quilt top the time passed, and before she realized it the grandfather clock beside the fireplace chimed six times. She laid aside her work and walked back onto the porch. She was beginning to get concerned. The idea of it getting dark without knowing about Gabel or Zebadiah was unsettling.

Suddenly she heard a noise coming from outside the kitchen. She hurried to the door, anxious for Zebadiah to be home. She opened the door just as Zebadiah staggered across the porch. His face and hair were covered with blood, and his clothes were dirty and torn.

"Let me see to your head," she said. "What happened? Good Lord, Zeb, what's happened?" She helped him into a chair at the table.

Zebadiah grabbed her arm and pulled her around until she was facing him. "Leave it be, girl." He wiped the blood from his face with the sleeve of his shirt. "Now you listen to me, girl. You listen good. You get yourself down the mountain. You get goin' now. You run now, you hear? And don't stop till you're clear of the mountain, where there's people that can help you." Zebadiah stopped long enough to wipe the blood that continued to pour from the side of his head. "Get goin', girl," he hissed.

"Ah can't leave you like this," she stammered. "Let me tend to your head."

Zebadiah jerked her arm away from his head. "Ah told you to get down the mountain and ah mean for you to obey."

"Where do you want me to go?" she screamed.

By this time Zebadiah was across the room, pulling down the gun he kept hanging over the fireplace. When she saw this she knew that whatever had happened to Zebadiah was more than he could handle. She grabbed her jacket from the hook beside the door and pulled it on.

"Are you sure, Zeb?" she asked one more time. "Maybe ah can help?"

Zebadiah raised his head slowly from where he sat holding the gun across his lap. "You find that preacher and you tell him Zebadiah Gaines sent these words. You tell him ah hold the blame for the evil ah brought into being and I hold the means of its destruction. Tell him ah'd 'preciate it if'n he'd pray my name to that Jesus he's always a talking 'bout 'cause ah expect to be seeing him soon an' ah intend on checkin' out them stories he's been talking about. Go on or it will be dark afore you get off the mountain, girl."

Earnestine turned to go.

"One more thing, girl. Ah'm right sorry 'bout the way I misused you. You don't have no need of shame. It was all me. You were a good wife and mama to my boys. And another thing, you take care of my boy Zack for me. Now get goin'."

Earnestine ran from the house to the path that led off the mountain. As she ran through trees and around rocks, she tried to think about what all of it meant but she couldn't. It took all of her concentration to keep from falling.

That had all happened four weeks earlier, and Earnestine had long since settled into the routine of caring for Silas and Reba Morgan's house. Silas had gone with the sheriff up the mountain where they'd found Gabel dead from a gunshot and Zebadiah beside him on the cabin floor, a hatchet buried in his chest.

Lester and his mom had helped Earnestine pack her belongings into the truck and deliver them to the Morgan home. There wasn't very much to pack, quilts and quilt tops, a few pieces of clothing, and several books.

Earnestine was at peace living in the Morgan home. She and Zack were close and every day she sat and listened while he read aloud from one of the books Lester Presley brought him. Lester showed up most days with something new for Zack or with a plan to take him fishing or just to have him spend the day helping Lester out on the farm. For the past thirty years Elvey Presley and Reba Morgan had met once a week and shared coffee, sweet rolls, and gossip.

"You know, Elvey, ah believe Lester has taken a real likin' to our Earnestine," Reba said while they sat munching on slices of lemon pound cake and washing it down with black coffee. Earnestine had baked the cake the evening before. Reba and Elvey were becoming spoiled by Earnestine's cooking, especially the sweets.

"Ah expect you might be right. He does seem to have a powerful lot of business over here since she came," Elvey answered. "It's about time he settled down and found someone special, and ah've been looking forward to being a grandma for a good many years."

"Earnestine's a fine young woman all right," Reba said. "She's traveled a rough road to womanhood, but ah believe she'll overcome all that in time."

Elvey nodded. "I wonder, is the ladies' class planning on fixin' baskets for the orphanage again this Christmas?" she asked. "This cake is mighty good."

"Earnestine, Earnestine child, can you come in here?" Reba called out. When Earnestine entered the room, Reba spoke again. "Come in here, child. Why don't you change your mind and join us? We're enjoying our coffee and this delicious cake you made."

"Look out, Earnestine," Elvey whispered when Earnestine sat down in the chair next to her. "She's up to something."

"Don't listen to her, child." Reba pretended outrage. "She just jealous 'cause your pound cake is better than hers." Reba patted Earnestine's leg and leaned close to whisper. "Don't tell Elvey but ah'm thinking you should be the official cake baker for the charity bake sale."

"Well, ah don't know." Earnestine laughed. "Ah wouldn't want to hurt anyone's feelings."

THE SEARCH ENDS
Chapter 18

"I just can't believe you did that," Judith said when Davis handed her the note with the address of the young man who had bought the ring from the pawn shop. "I'll call Ida Mae and tell her we may be close to finding Mama's ring." She picked up the phone to dial but stopped. "No, I think I'll wait. I'll surprise her once we actually have it."

Davis watched his wife of thirty years jump around like a little kid with the news that the search for her mama's ring might soon be over. "I thought we'd drive up and see the boy next week. It's not that far from here, only a couple hundred miles. It'll be a nice drive. We can make it a mini-vacation."

"That sounds good." Judith answered. "This is so exciting, finally finding the ring after all it's been through."

They decided to drive up the next Wednesday. "I checked with Triple A and there are no hotels in Deer Creek, Kentucky. The closest hotel is a Holiday Inn Express in Corbin twenty miles away," Davis said before they left.

During the drive, Davis tried again to talk about his experience at the mission in Portland, but he couldn't find the words to put with his feelings about the work or the people there. He thought part of it might worrying about how Judith would see his sudden interest in working with the city's outcasts. In the end the drive passed without him mentioning it. This brought on another bout of guilt for his lack of commitment and courage. They arrived in Corbin and checked into the motel.

"Deer Creek is about twenty miles out, I reckon," the hotel clerk explained. "You take the main road to Highway 27 North till you reach the stop sign. Turn left there and go about five miles till the black top ends. Stay on the graveled road for about another fifteen miles and it'll take you into Deer Creek. The road don't go no place else so you can't get lost. You got friends or relations there? Ain't many outsiders ever go there."

"Well, actually, I'm looking for a Lester Presley," Davis explained. He's a friend of a friend."

"Don't reckon ah know him. Ah do know there's a preacher over there named Presley. He might be kin to this here Lester. He's got a church over to Deer Creek. It's on the main road if I remember right. Ah hear tell it's Holiness or something like that. You know, the snake handlers."

Davis shrugged. "I don't know anything about that, but we'll check it out when we get there. Maybe the preacher can help."

Davis and Judith reached the Deer Creek Holiness Church just as the Wednesday evening service began. They stayed for the service. Both were more than a little curious about the snake handlers, but they need not have worried. This was Wednesday prayer meeting and no snakes were present, only a great deal of praying, shouting, and testifying.

As soon as the service ended, they made their way to the front of the church, where the preacher stood talking to several other men." Excuse me, my name is Davis Barnes and I wonder if I might have a word with you?"

"Good evening and welcome to Deer Creek. Ah hope you enjoyed the service?" Homer Presley held out his hand to Davis. "How can I help you?"

"I'm looking for a young man named Lester Presley," Davis said.

A young man standing next to the preacher spoke up. "I'm Lester Presley. Can I help you?"

Davis began telling the story of the ring and Judith's search for it. Judith stood by quietly as Davis talked; then she looked at Lester. "It's my mama's ring. I really want it back."

Lester talked with Judith for a few minutes then excused himself. "Oh Davis, I don't think he's going to be willing to give up the ring!" she cried.

Before Davis could answer, Lester returned. He reached for Judith's hand and slipped the ring inside. "I believe this belongs to you, ma'am," he said shyly.

Judith looked down at the ring. The light from the bare electric light bulb hanging from the ceiling sparkled off the black stone. "Oh, my, my goodness, it is really Mama's ring. Oh look, Davis. Look. I finally have Mama's ring back." Judith began to cry, burying her face in Davis's shoulder. "I thought I'd never see it again. Wait till I tell Ida Mae."

Davis pulled two hundred-dollar bills from his pocket and offered them to Lester, who shook his head and backed away from his outstretched hand.

"No, no, I don't want your money. I'm just happy to help."

Within a few moments Judith had the ring tucked safely inside her purse.

Harmon Presley, who was standing nearby, spoke up. "All good things come to those that love the Lord. Unto everything there is a season, a time to sow and a time to reap."

The preacher's words caused Davis to, again, remember his mama and her deep faith in God and his protection.

Later, as Davis and Judith drove back home, they chatted happily.

"Davis," Judith said. "I'm going to give Mama's ring to Ida Mae. She should be the one to hold it. She has a special feeling for it that I don't have. I mean, I love the idea that it belonged to Mama and all, but I never really saw her wear it. I guess it just means more to Ida Mae."

"I'm glad, honey. I think you're right." He looked across the front seat to where Judith sat looking out the window, and for a while they rode in silence.

Davis thought back over the years he'd been married to the woman sitting in the seat beside him. He remembered all the bad things God had brought them through as well as the good life God had given to them. After a while he said, "Judith, honey, I want to talk to you about my life. I'm going to make a change."

He began to tell Judith about the Safe House Mission and the feeling he had that God was leading him into a change in his life. As he talked Davis had the feeling that his mama was watching and nodding her approval of his decision.

CPSIA information can be obtained
at www.ICGtesting.com
Printed in the USA
LVOW04s2050281216
519036LV00009B/38/P